SPICY BITES

LEATHER

2020

ROMANCE
WRITERS
of Australia

Leather 2020: Spicy Bites Anthology

Anthology of Short Stories published by the Romance Writers of Australia Inc ©2020

Print ISBN: 978-0-6485877-6-7

Digital ISBN: 978-0-6485877-7-4

Spicy Bites Coordinator: Jillian Jones

Cover Design: Louisa West

Edited by Wendy Davies and Dannielle Line

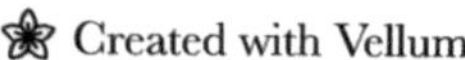 Created with Vellum

SPICY BITES

LEATHER
Short Story Anthology
2020

Contents

Stevie Nicks sang to Don Henley "Give to me your leather, take from me my lace."

Leather. The very sound of the word takes the imagination in a steamy direction. It's strong, it's supple, it's soft and above all, leather is supremely sexy. A leather jacket on a bad bad boy teamed with snug well-worn denim and a little stubble, strong leather-clad thighs, the feel of leather against soft skin…sigh.

This year we challenged our authors to write erotic short stories incorporating the theme of leather – and wow, they have delivered in spades! Our winning stories are so hot they positively sizzle. But don't take my word for it, indulge yourself in the sexy stories they've created within these pages.

So, without further ado, I'm pleased to present to you this year's collection of Spicy Bites – Leather. Enjoy…

Regards

Joanne Tracey

President 2020

Cuffed

KRISTINE CHARLES

/kʌft/

verb: taken, have a boyfriend, girlfriend, significant other
the Urban Dictionary

Benjamin Leigh hurried up the otherwise ordinary street on the outskirts of the city, dodging the occasional passer-by in the peak-hour crush. He'd been glad to get out of the office at a decent time tonight, having worked stupid hours over the past few weeks to finish the latest campaign proposal for his biggest client. He'd pitched the concept less than an hour ago and—*thank fuck*—they'd loved it. Once they'd signed the contracts, he'd hung around for thirty minutes of glad-handling and a quick celebratory beer, then he was out the door. He needed a night off.

And a night to get off.

Which is why he was heading for The Club.

Turning into a small alleyway, he pushed open the narrow black door to his left. Inside, he pulled his membership card from his wallet, holding it out for the maître'd to peruse. The man glanced down at the card and back up at

Benjamin before waving him through the second door. Once inside, Benjamin paused, letting his eyes adjust to the dimmer lighting.

The Club on a Wednesday night was a little quieter than usual. Only about half of the stately wingback chairs and overstuffed leather couches spread through the large room were occupied. Being mid-week, the play was also more discreet, and no one had yet moved to the back corner of the room where The Club laid out their more *interesting* furniture. At the bar, there were only a few—

Whoa.

Benjamin hesitated, running a hand through his hair as he took in the woman sitting alone on a stool at the end of the bar. How anyone made being perched on one of those look elegant he didn't know but, somehow, she pulled it off. She sat at a slight angle to the bar, with a straight back, one slender leg crossed over the other, and the thin heel of her shoe hooked over the rung of the stool. The fingers of her right hand were wrapped around the stem of a wine glass that rested on the bar in front of her, the garnet coloured liquid inside incandescent under the spotlights overhead.

She exuded power.

There was something oddly familiar about her.

And she was looking straight at him.

He made it to the bar without losing all coherent thought, putting the familiarity down to the fact he worked with powerful women all the time, and ordered a single-malt whisky, peaty and neat. He felt the woman studying him as he took the first sip. Her stare burned into the side of his face.

He couldn't help but turn towards her.

"Hello."

"Hello," she replied, her eyes dark in the muted light of the club.

He took another sip, his once-over catching on the small, plain, crown-shaped pin attached to her dress. The Club issued these plain pins to those who preferred a dominant role. Those who were more permanent Dominants wore a crown embellished with a coloured jewel, depending on their preferences.

Her eyes widened slightly as her gaze slid over the lapels of his suit coat. He did not wear a crown.

"You're submissive?"

He shook his head, enjoying the honeyed tones of her voice. "A bottom."

She nodded. "Masochist?"

"No."

She nodded again. "Good. You here to play?"

"Yes."

"What did you have in mind?"

He let his lips curve in a grin even as his heart raced. "Well, that would be up to you."

"That it would," she said with a throaty chuckle, her frank admiration blazing a path over his body.

He all but quivered with excitement.

"How about I restrain you, then make you come?"

He had to admit, after the week he'd had, that sounded pretty fucking fabulous. "Please."

"What's your safe word?"

"Lettuce."

"Lettuce?"

He shrugged as she raised an eyebrow, perfectly arched over dark eyes.

"Okay then. Lettuce." She reached forward, toying with the blood red tie loosely knotted at his neck. "May I?"

"Yes."

She tugged at his tie, working the knot before pulling it free and tucking it into the pocket of her dress. He helped her with the buttons of his dress shirt, tugging it from his shoulders as she unbuttoned and unzipped his suit pants, pushing them to the floor. He quickly toed off his shoes and stepped out of the pants.

"Leave them," she said as he bent to pull off his socks and gather his clothes, her tone brooking no argument. "Follow me."

Follow her he did.

And it was an exceptional view. The woman was tall, her height aided by the high, shiny black stilettos she wore on her feet. Her long, lithe body was sheathed in a port wine coloured dress, the fabric hugging every dip and curve, but leaving her arms and lower legs bare. She'd twisted her mahogany hair into some sort of knot at the base of her neck. And she moved with a feline grace, winding through the lounges and tables set out across the floor towards the dark wood and leather shackles of the St Andrew's Cross.

Well, yes, and please.

It only took a subtle tilt of her head for him to be turning, pressing his lower back to the centre of the Cross. Her fingers were nimble as she worked the fastenings of the attached cuffs, threading the heavy leather through the metal buckle and pulling it just tight enough. By the time she'd both his wrists and ankles restrained, his cock was half-mast, pushing against the cotton of his boxer-briefs, begging to be freed.

She knew it too, her eyes warm with laughter as she looked up at him, her hand deliberately brushing against his cock.

"Not yet."

He all but whimpered as her hand fell away.

She took a long moment to study him. "Your safe word

is lettuce, and you'll use yellow if you need me to slow down."

"Yes."

"Except for those two words you may not speak."

He nodded.

"Excellent." She grinned and lifted a finger, trailing the tip along his collarbone to the notch in his throat, pressing there ever so slightly. "I'm going to make you work for it."

He swallowed and her grin widened as she leaned towards him, poking out her tongue to lick along the column of his neck.

"Okay?"

At her murmur, he nodded again, and she brought her lips to his neck, sucking so sharply he knew she'd leave a mark.

He didn't mind.

Neither did his cock, which was now at full attention and weeping against his shorts.

"You like that," she murmured, pressing her hip against his dick. "I can tell."

The smart-arse response was on the tip of his tongue, but he bit it back, swallowing the words and a moan as she pinched his nipples.

"Good job."

She let her fingers play over his chest, trailing further down his belly, exploring the ridges of his torso. His muscles jumped as she scratched at him, her manicured nails leaving a light trail of red against his skin, and the soft huff of her responding chuckle brushing against his neck.

"Not a masochist," she murmured. "But you don't mind a little pain."

She wasn't wrong.

His hips pressed forward, wrists straining against the

leather cuffs as she trailed her fingernails down the centre of his chest and torso. More faint red lines lead to the band of his underwear and dipped beneath. She wrapped her hand firmly around his shaft before she tugged him free from the cotton and his hips surged forward, keen for any relief.

She gave nothing away, idly running her fist over the length of him, watching as the head of his cock popped through the ring of her thumb and forefinger. A few people gathered to watch them, the sight of a six-foot-three-inch man in leather cuffs secured to the St Andrew's Cross not a common occurrence in the club. She ignored the soft murmurs and moans of their audience, tightening her fist and eliciting a garbled groan.

"Good boy."

His eyes widened as she sank to her knees.

"Just because it's attached to you, doesn't mean it's yours. At least…" A foil packet materialised in her hand and she ripped it open with her teeth. "Not right now."

Jesus.

He hadn't expected she'd—

Fuck.

He wasn't going to say no.

She licked her lips as she sheathed him with the thin latex, eyes lifted to his from beneath heavy lashes. "May I?"

His lips were already parting to form the words—*yes, fuck yes*—when he remembered he didn't have permission to speak. Instead, he nodded frantically, his chin almost hitting his chest on the downstroke, only to be rewarded with another throaty laugh.

"I'll take that as a yes."

She ran her fist over him twice more before leaning in and resting the head of his cock against her bottom lip, her tongue pressing against him. She lapped at his dick a few times before sliding it into her mouth and—

"Mmfgfhfhfhgggh," he moaned, teeth clenched tightly shut to prevent his words escaping.

She worked him slowly, bringing him in and out of her mouth with a steady rhythm, moving him deeper with each stroke. She was clearly in no rush.

He was in no rush either. The heat of her mouth, the pressure of her tongue, the scrape of her teeth. They felt… what was the word for the feeling that started at the base of your spine and spread tingling along every nerve?

Oh yeah.

Spectacular.

He glanced down, appreciating the view of having a woman on her knees at his feet when she lifted her eyes to his, mouth still stretched around the girth of his cock and——

Holy shit.

"Vicky?"

The minute the word fell from his mouth, he knew he'd broken something. Her eyes narrowed immediately, and she pulled her luscious lips from his shaft, sitting back on her heels. "It's Victoria," she said, and the underlying chill in her voice would have frozen vodka. "Or Ma'am to you."

He nodded.

Even in that position, kneeling at his feet and with her lips swollen from his cock, she still oozed power, but now her eyes were clouded with a question.

How do you know me?

He wasn't sure he should answer it, at least not until she verbalised it.

Anyway, he still wasn't allowed to speak, and he wasn't going to give her any more reason to be irritated with him.

As he waited, she glanced back at his throbbing dick, its shaft streaked with her dark lipstick. Her forehead was furrowed in deep lines and he knew, even before she stood from her crouch and unbuckled the leather around his wrists, he wouldn't be coming any time soon.

Damn.

"Unbuckle your feet," she said, once she'd finished with his wrists.

His fingers were clumsy as he worked at the leather, pulling, and pushing to free the restraints. His dick, although deflating, wasn't quite on board with the hiatus in activity and needed to be shoved back into his underwear so it wasn't bobbing in the breeze.

A bobbing cock was never an attractive sight.

By the time he'd freed his legs, she'd taken a seat in a corner of the lounge area. The space was lit only by the light from a bare bulb hanging from one of those arty, industrial type lamps standing between two wingback chairs. He crossed to her, still only wearing his underwear but now carrying his socks because, well, a man almost naked but for jocks and socks looked stupid. As he moved closer, he noticed the pile of clothes on the chair across from her, the nervous twitch in the leg she'd crossed over her knee, and the ever-deepening furrow in her brow.

"Benjamin Leigh, right?"

He nodded, hesitating as he considered where he should sit.

She inclined her head towards the chair opposite.

"You're Vick—Victoria Daniels."

She nodded. "I am."

Victoria suited her now. She was too polished to be a Vicky, despite what they'd called her at school. "Well," he shrugged as he pulled on his pants and sat. "How have you been?"

Silence stretched between them for a long moment until she let out a sharp bark of laughter, this one harsher and more cutting than her earlier throaty chuckle. "It's been a long time."

"It has." It'd been over fifteen years since he'd seen Victoria Daniels and, while she had the same eyes, she'd looked a lot different at seventeen.

A whole lot different.

"Vicky, Vicky," Ben ran down the corridor. "Wait up."

He pushed through the masses of students spilling out of the classrooms and into the corridors in a Pavlovian response to the final bell. The weekend was here, and the St Ignatius High students couldn't get to it fast enough.

"Oh, hey," Vicky said, turning to face him and clutching her folder to her chest. "Sorry. I didn't hear you."

But the way she said it…He knew she *had* heard him. Weird but, whatever. He bent down and pressed his lips to the blunt fringe of straight, light brown hair covering her forehead. "No worries. Are we still hanging out tonight?"

"Uh," Vicky hesitated, the toe of her battered sandshoe scuffing at the ground.

His stomach sank to his feet. What was going on?

"I can't tonight. Mum and Dad…" Her voice caught on the words. "But we need to talk."

"Are your parents still giving you a hard time about us?"

"No." She shook her head. "Well, not…It's me. I think…Maybe they're—"

He held up his hand. "Don't say it. They're not fucking right. We're not too young. We'll be fine."

"I have to," she replied, and he winced at the sound of her cracking voice. "I can't keep doing this—"

"Doing what?" he asked, his voice hardening.

"We shouldn't talk about it here."

She turned away from him and he grabbed a fistful of her Radiohead t-shirt, spinning her to face him again. "Why not? You said you wanted to talk to me. So, talk."

"Shit," Vicky mumbled under her breath. "I didn't…I don't…Not here."

"Are you breaking up with me?"

"No. Just…Maybe," she glanced at the folder she had clasped to her chest. "I just…I don't know…I think maybe we should take a break."

A break?

"Is there someone else?"

"No!" she replied, her eyes widening in surprise. "I would never."

This morning he'd have taken her at her word. But now…he wasn't sure what to believe.

"But you think we should take a break?"

"Well," she focused on the ground again, her toe making small circles on the battered linoleum floor. "Yeah. I guess. Maybe."

"Fine then," he shrugged. "Whatever you want."

"But…I—"

She'd been talking to his back. He hadn't waited to hear what she'd said.

***

"What have you been up to?" Benjamin asked before rubbing a hand over his jaw to hide his sigh. Could he be any more inane?

Fuck, this was awkward.

"A little of this, a little of that," she replied, not really saying anything. "You?"

"Same," he said, with a nod and an uncomfortable glance around the room.

"You're a lawyer?" he asked. She had always wanted to be a lawyer, like her Dad.

"No, that…" she shook her head. "That didn't work out. I'm a stockbroker."

He laughed. "What? You hated numbers, and you hated business studies. What's that about?"

She laughed with him, giving a shrug of her shoulders as she relaxed some. "The world, and my career choices, moved in mysterious ways. And I like shoes. What about you? Art?"

"Kind of. Advertising," he replied. "But Account Management now. Not creative."

"Oh. You still draw?"

He shook his head. He hadn't picked up a pencil in years.

"Oh."

A waiter passed by and they both ordered sparkling water—with lemon for him and cucumber for her.

"We're both very different people now than we were," she observed.

That was stating the obvious. "We are."

"Maybe we should have talked before…" She waved towards the St Andrew's Cross across the room.

And that was stating the truth. "Well, yeah…But," he shrugged. "I didn't recognise you."

"I'm not seventeen anymore."

"No, you're not."

"Neither are you."

He didn't mind her appreciative contemplation of his chest. "No."

"I've resolved my issues around needing to be a good girl."

He chuckled. "I can see that."

"I'm not scared of commitment. Not anymore. But now…you come here…you seem…" She seemed unclear about what she wanted to say. "I'm sorry. That may be presumptuous. But I'm sorry if I did that to you."

Those words surprised him, and he hesitated. Was he scared of commitment? Or was she? "No, I—"

"It's okay," she said, cutting him off. "I am sorry. I didn't know what I was doing in high school and, well, I didn't want to repeat my parents' mistakes."

"But your parents were happily married—"

"No." She shook her head. "They separated the…uh. They told me Dad was moving out the day we…"

"Oh."

He didn't know what to say. Her parents had also been high school sweethearts, had met on their first day at St Ignatius, had married less than a year after graduation. Had Vicky—Victoria—less than a year after they finished university. Unlike his own parents, they'd been a model couple.

"I'm sorry."

"Long time ago now," She shrugged. "I've had a while to adjust. But I didn't handle it well at first. My parents had been together for so many years I thought they were invincible and…well…clearly, they weren't. So…I thought maybe we weren't."

Ben nodded. It made some sort of sense now. At least, it made as much sense as angsty teenage decisions could make some fifteen years later. When they were older and wiser and…

Yeah. Still wanted to fuck each other's brains out.

"I've never been scared of commitment," he said, sliding to his knees and moving towards her. "But maybe I didn't understand it required more than just determination. My parents—"

"I know—"

He held up a hand. "My parents were terrible together, and I was determined to do better. I thought it would just happen through sheer force of will and..." He trailed off as she reached towards him, her fingers pressing against his mouth.

"Can we get out of here? I live around the corner."

"Yes."

Thank fuck.

Her place was, quite literally, around the corner.

And it was stunning.

As she led him towards the stairs, he got glimpses of the light wood floors, white walls and exposed, latte coloured brick, all very fresh and sophisticated. But the living area was nothing on the main bedroom and the imposing wrought-iron bed set against a wall of bricks behind the bedhead.

Before he could comment, Victoria pulled another pair of leather cuffs from a bedside drawer.

"May I?"

He nodded, holding out his hands.

She buckled them quickly, restraining his wrists before pushing him back onto the bed. "On your back, in the middle."

He wriggled into the centre of the bed, his head on the pillows, and she took his hands, lifting them over his head and clipping the cuffs to the headboard.

"Custom bed?" he asked, shifting around to get comfortable.

"Nope. Bought it at Freedom," she laughed, turning her attention to his shirt buttons.

"Of course you did," he said, his back arching with pleasure as she pushed the sides of his shirt apart and pinched his nipple.

"No more talking," she said, moving on to unbuckle his belt and unfasten his pants. "Not unless you use your safe words, which are?"

"Lettuce and yellow," he replied, raising his hips as she pulled his pants and boxers down and off.

"Excellent."

She reached into the side table drawer and pulled out a condom, ripping open the foil and sheathing him quickly. Then, without any further ado, she bent forward and slid his cock between her lips.

His hips responded instinctively, lifting off the bed. *Jesus.* Her mouth was hot and wet and—

"Uh, uh," she said, her thumb and forefinger circling the base of his cock and squeezing, while her other hand firmly cupped his balls. "Behave."

Anything you say.

He tensed his stomach, pressing his arse into the soft mattress as she continued working his cock deeper into her mouth, the room full of her quiet sucking sounds and his stifled moans. He fought the fluttering of his eyelids, desperate to watch her head as it moved, her hair still in its tidy knot. It allowed him to see the hollow in her cheeks as she sucked, the freckles scatted across her nose which reddened as she took more of him into her mouth.

Then, suddenly, that warm, cosy wetness was gone.

Thankfully, his fuzzy brain prevented him from speaking fully formed words and, instead, garbled sounds fell from his lips.

"You think this is all about you?" she asked with a

breathless laugh, sliding off the bed, her arms twisted behind her. "No, no, no."

The dark red dress dropped away to reveal a beautiful lace bodysuit thing which, he was sure, had some flouncy French name. He couldn't care less. It was pale pink and sheer enough that the dark rose of her nipples peeked through from beneath the fragile fabric. Nipples he was keen to taste. And it hinted of other secrets hidden beneath, secrets he was also eager to learn.

She wasn't going to make him wait.

Another twist of her arms behind her and she was sliding the straps from her shoulders, easing the delicate lace over her hips and kicking it away.

She paused then, taking a long moment to look at him. He wondered what she was thinking, her brow slightly creased even as her eyes burned with arousal. Arousal that only served to stoke his, his cock full and throbbing where it lay against his belly.

The moment passed, and she was climbing onto the bed, throwing her leg over his hips and straddling him, her body rising over him and her hair still in that ridiculously neat knot.

She was glorious.

Ever so slowly, she took hold of his erection, pointing it towards the ceiling and raising herself over it. Her heat radiated against the head of his cock, even through the thin layer of rubber, and his hips thrust upwards, wanting that wet heat surrounding his dick.

Her firm fist squeezing his shaft halted him.

"Always so greedy," she murmured, waiting until he relaxed back into the mattress before sinking down on him, taking him into her.

Fuck she felt good.

They'd had sex when they were younger. Quick,

youthful fumblings when they'd had no real idea what they were doing, and he'd been more focused on trying not to come than on whether she was enjoying it.

It surprised him how quickly that sensation of impending embarrassment returned as she'd taken him inside her. Clenching his eyes closed, he started counting backwards from one hundred in sevens. It was a desperate attempt to stave off a rapid end to proceedings as Victoria moved over him, slowly rocking back and forth on his cast iron dick.

"Open your eyes," she said, her words a clear demand as her fingers played over his lips. "Open wide."

And he did, eyelids fluttering open and peering up at her.

"You were counting backwards in sevens, weren't you?" she said, hands now braced against his chest as she moved. "You always did that, you know."

He nodded.

"You used to mumble the numbers," she said with a sigh as she sped up, rubbing herself against him. "One hundred, ninety-three, eighty-six, seventy-nine—"

"Seventy-two," he said with a laugh and thrust his hips, pressing himself deeper into her.

The resulting gasp, air catching hard in her throat, pleased him, and he did it again.

She didn't stop him, didn't scold him for speaking.

So, he thrust up a third time.

"Yes," she groaned, fingers contracting and nails digging into his pecs. "Yes."

Pulling his knees up and gripping the bedframe in his cuffed hands, he dug his heels into the mattress, using the leverage to drive into her from beneath, his hips setting a relentless rhythm. As he did so, she leaned back against his thighs, her finger playing against her clit and her writhing in his lap causing her boobs to bounce in the most attractive way.

"Don't you dare stop," she muttered. "Don't you dare."

And why would he? The feel of her hot and tight around him was the most indulgent feeling, driving him higher and higher and higher until—

"Fuck, yes," she moaned, falling forward, and pressing her hands to his stomach, grinding herself on his dick. "Fuck. Yes."

He didn't hold himself back, thrusting harder, the metal fastenings on the leather cuffs clinking as he released into the condom with a groan, his belly muscles vibrating against her hands.

He wanted to tell her *no, stay* as she slid his still semi-rigid cock from inside her. She slid the condom from his dick and flinging it over the bed into what he assumed was a bin.

At least he hoped it was.

Dealing with spilled semen on her shagpile rug would not be fun.

Releasing his hands, and settling against him, Victoria tucked her forehead against his neck, and he wrapped his arms around her. He hadn't had a chance to hold her. It brought back memories of the way they'd lay out on the sunlounge in her yard back in the day, even though they'd not been naked and sweaty back then.

"May I…" he began, his voice raspy and rough.

"You may," she said, the nodding of her head causing her cheek to slide against his shoulder.

"Maybe I have been a little…" he hesitated, avoiding any use of the word scared. "A little reluctant to consider commitment since…But that's not your fault. My parents didn't set the best example and while I always thought I was different…always wanted to be different, there was some stuff I needed to work through before—"

"How did you wind up at The Club?" she asked, cutting him off.

He shrugged. "Nothing too complicated. I like being restrained. Occasionally I like being spanked or cropped. I'd prefer the people doing that have some idea about what they're doing, so I found The Club. How about you?"

She laughed again, and he revelled in it. He'd forgotten how much he'd loved her laugh.

"I'm a female, and I work in stockbroking. Occasionally, I like to work out my frustrations against the male species on a willing bloke."

Now, it was his turn to laugh. "I can understand that."

"But seriously," she continued. "I like to be in control. It's something I've learned, but it works for me now—"

"I like it."

She lifted her head, bracing her chin on her hand. "You do?"

"I do."

"Okay then."

She paused, taking a long moment to let her gaze slide over his face. Then she shifted, pulling herself up and over him, and bringing her lips down to press against his.

Her lips were still soft, like he remembered, but now they moved with the wisdom of age. The occasional slick of her tongue or nip of her teeth blended with the gentle press of her mouth as she moved. And while her taste was familiar, it was completely new, like the difference between a young whisky and a well-aged one.

He'd always preferred his single malts on the older side.

After a while, Victoria pulled away, folding her arms over his chest and propping her chin on her hands. "Are we good?" she asked, her forehead furrowing as she looked at him.

He nodded. "Yeah. We're good."

A YEAR LATER

Dearest Benjamin.

He grinned as he read the small card tucked into the ribbon of the gift box he held in his hand.

In honour of our first re-meeting, and your predilection for leather cuffs, what better present to give you on our wedding day than this.

See you at the church. I'll be the one in white.

Victoria.

Pulling the black-wrapped box free of its white ribbon, Ben tore the paper off, letting it fall to the floor. He lifted the lid and found…not what he expected. Inside, instead of some heavy leather cuff, there was an understated bracelet of the softest calfskin leather cord, knotted and looped through two joined rings, one muted platinum and one black ceramic.

The rings matched the wedding bands they'd chosen—his black, and platinum for her.

He laughed. For his wedding gift to her, Ben stole the key to her leather cuffs and commissioned a jeweller and a locksmith work their magic to create an intricately designed key pendant. They inlaid the head with diamonds and a practical blade, which worked to unlock the cuffs. The result, hanging from a fine platinum chain, was exquisite.

Clearly cuffs—leather or otherwise—would forever be their *thing*.

A sharp knock at the door had him quickly tossing the box aside and sliding the bracelet onto his wrist, tugging down the sleeve of his shirt and suit coat. A quick smoothing of his pink tie—Victoria had repeatedly told him it was blush, but the bloody thing was pink—and he was ready, eager to get started.

The sooner they completed the formalities, the sooner they could get the honeymoon underway.

And the sooner he could get cuffed again.

The Winning Captain

KAREN LIEVERSZ

"We've found you a wife," says my mother in her imperious, *don't mess with me*, tone.

I curl my fingers around the cricket ball in my pocket, the smooth leather gliding across the sensitive skin of my pads. It quietens the panic that slams into my chest like a short ball off the pitch. Fury quickly follows but respect for my parents is ingrained in me and I squash the urge to snap. Instead, I take a deep breath.

"I'm not ready to get married yet. I'm only twenty-four."

"You have a responsibility to carry on the family name," says my father in his, *you've got no say in this, do as you're told*, voice.

Mother purses her lips, her hands going to her hips as she glares up at me from her five feet two inches. "Your father had two children at your age."

I clench my teeth. "I can find my own wife."

"Really? When was the last time you brought a girl home to meet us? Let me think."

She closes her eyes and scrunches up her face before snapping her shrewd gaze back to mine.

"That's right. Never! You spend all your time at that club playing cricket. I'm going to die without any grandchildren."

"That's not true. You've got grandchildren."

"Not from our only son," replies my father, his tone unyielding.

A knock at the front door saves me. "I'll get it." I bolt from the room, the threatening chime of wedding bells resounding in my head.

I wrench the door open and time stops. My old friend, Michael, stands on the threshold. I shake my head, wondering if I've succumbed to the sweltering humidity, and he's a hallucination. But no. It's Michael. And he looks good. Too good. Dark curls peak out rebelliously from the baseball cap on his head. He's wearing fitted cream trousers and a navy-blue polo shirt that clings to his chest. I do a double take at the ink swirling down his arms, swallowing up the creamy smoothness. That's new.

"Hello, Ashan." His voice is a soft, lazy drawl, just like I remember.

"Michael," I swallow. "This is a surprise."

He gives me a wry smile. "I should have called on you earlier, but..."

"No, no." I respond. "You don't owe me any explanations."

Michael returned home last month after being abroad for the last five years to help his father on their family's tea plantation. He's even started playing club cricket for Kandy. That's how I knew he was back. My parents haven't said anything, but I know they're hurt he stayed overseas so long. Hurt he hasn't contacted them since his return. They'd understand if they knew what had happened during our final school year—something they can never find out.

He cocks an eyebrow at me. "Are you going to invite me in?"

"Of course. Sorry. Where are my manners?" I move aside.

Heat radiates from him as he steps into the foyer and a jolt of awareness rips through my body. I tell myself it's nerves, the memory of our uneasy parting still etched in my mind like the ink covering his arms.

"Amma, Thatha, look who's here?" I say as I usher Michael into our living room.

My father shakes his hand, frowning at the tattoos for a moment before widening his smile in greeting.

Mother pecks him on both cheeks. "Michael, you're looking well. No doubt you've had all the young women of England falling over each other for your attention."

A blush creeps up his neck. "I've been too busy with Uni and then work, Aunty."

"Of course, you have," says Father with a wink before offering him a whiskey.

Mother rushes into the kitchen and returns a few minutes later with cake.

"I've missed this," says Michael with a sigh, crumbs spilling down his chin. "They don't make love cake like this in England."

My mother beams at him. Michael is like a second son to my parents, having spent as much time in our home as he did in his own when we were growing up. That's why his absence has been all the more hurtful.

"Are you back for good?" my father asks.

His eyes flick to me. "Maybe, Uncle. It depends."

"Well, I hope you stay. You've been gone too long. I

take it you're in Colombo for the cricket final this weekend?"

Michael's fingers drum on the side of the chair, his gaze dropping to the floor. "Yes, I…umm…I'm the captain."

I choke on my whiskey. "What?" I exclaim as I jump out of the chair, coughing.

His face tenses as he answers. "Our team's captain was struck down with hepatitis. He won't recover in time for the match."

I shove a hand into my pocket and clasp the cricket ball with clammy fingers. "Why would they put a newcomer into the team as captain? Shouldn't it have gone to the Vice-Captain?"

He gives me a small smile. "Normally, yes…but…"

"With your reputation and international experience, they asked you to do it," my father finishes for him.

"Yes."

He laughs. "That's going to be a bit awkward, what with Ashan being captain of the Colombo team."

Michael nods.

I squeeze the cricket ball, needing its solidity as I process what this means. Colombo has been the best performing team all season. Until Michael joined them, the Kandy team hadn't been a threat. If we were to lose now, when everyone assumes we'll win, I could lose the captaincy.

My parents pepper Michael with questions for the next hour. I fidget in my seat as I think about his prowess on the cricket field. He's faster, stronger, smarter than I am. Despite my fears, I relax as his familiar drawl fills the room. Cricket was what bound us. When we were young, we'd play tennis ball cricket in the street. Then later, as teens, we'd be forever at the nets practicing together. It feels good to have him back home. Like old times. The times before a wall as thick as a boa tree came between us.

When my mother brings up the subject of girls again, Michael springs out of his chair.

"Sorry, Aunty, but I should get going." He bounces on his heels. "Ashan, one of the things I've missed since coming back home is McDonalds. Would you like to come have a bite with me?"

The ball I still hold in my pocket is slippery with sweat. *Should I?* We were good friends once. There's no reason we can't be again. Besides, it will save me from any further *wife* discussions, at least for today.

"Sure, I'd love to."

It's a twenty-minute walk and we indulge in benign chit chat, pretending that nothing has happened—not the last five years, nor the awkward incident, or our lost friendship.

It's mid-week and McDonalds is quiet. We've barely sat down when two girls, dressed in skin-tight jeans and tank tops approach us.

"Captain," they purr at me.

It's March in Colombo; no matter how sexy they think they look in their jeans, they'd have to be sweating like paddy field workers in the hot sun underneath the thick fabric. Bright smiles turn to angry frowns when we wave them on, ignoring their muffled 'must be gay' grumbles.

I'd be amused at their disappointment if I wasn't annoyed by it. Women used to give me a wide berth thanks to the six-inch scar burned down my right cheek—a mugging gone wrong when I was sixteen. Not anymore. My scar seems to have become invisible to the ladies. They all want to score with the Captain.

We scoff down our Big Macs and move onto the fries, enjoying the companionable silence. It's comfortable. Familiar. I steal a fry from Michael's packet and earn myself a slap on the wrist. I grin at him, and he grins back. I've missed hanging out with him. He's my machan, my mate. The man who knows me better than anyone.

"Why d'you get the tattoos?" I ask.

He smirks, "You like them?"

"They're pretty cool."

"I've got them all over my front and back too. I'd be happy to show you."

His eyes glitter at me and just like that I'm a teenager again. The cords on his neck stand out. It's the only sign he's tensed, that he knows he's crossed the line.

I lower my eyes and grab another chip. This is the reason we haven't seen each other in five years.

It was a couple of days before the school big match. We'd been practicing in the nets and had headed off to the shower block. Everyone else had gone home. Michael had given me a playful punch in the stomach. I'd play punched him back in the chest. When we'd arrived at the showers, we were still grappling with each other. He took a cricket ball, slipped it down my pants and pressed it against my crotch.

Our eyes locked; the smell of earth, sweat and leather engulfing us. My dick swelled under the pressure of the cricket ball and the heat of Michael's gaze. A guttural moan broke the spell.

Michael cleared his throat and yanked his hand from my pants. "Sorry, Ashan. I shouldn't have done that."

"It's okay," I replied, my brain frozen. What else could I say? We were best friends. We did everything together. Well…almost everything.

He gave me a tight smile. "I still shouldn't have done it. I know you don't swing that way."

I laughed and gave him a cheeky grin, desperate to break the tension. "How do you know I don't?"

He chuckled. "Because when we get naked, I know you're gonna be keeping that dick and arse of yours out of my line of sight. It's a work of magic the way you manage to hide your privates from me when we're all wet and soapy."

My face burned at the hunger in his eyes. I didn't think he'd noticed. It wasn't because I was afraid that he'd jump me or anything. I shielded myself because I was confused at the tingling sensations washing over me when we showered together. The tightening of my groin. If he'd seen it, our friendship would have been ruined. I wasn't gay. But he was my best friend, and he was gay. He was ripped, even back then. I admired his muscles. That was all it was. Admiration. I was a teenager. Teenage boys threw boners over everything. Didn't they? Still, our friendship wasn't the same afterwards.

"So, your parents look good."

A few seconds pass before his words soak in. I clear my throat. "Yeah. Mother's happy with her government job. Father works too many hours, but he seems to get a real kick out of delivering babies."

"Great. That's great." He clenches his hands. "And have you found yourself a girl to settle down with?"

I scowl. "No, but my parents say they've found me one." I lower my voice, as if whispering will make it less true. "They want me to meet her."

Michael's gaze narrows. "This is the twenty-first century. They can't make you marry."

I shiver. I wish it was that easy, but I fear it won't be. I slip the cricket ball out of my pocket and roll it around in my hand, needing the familiar smoothness of the new leather to settle my nerves.

"Why didn't you come back after you finished Uni?" I blurt out.

Michael's face darkens and I immediately wish I could take back the words. He leans across the table. "You know why."

I panic, dropping the ball. He picks it up and holds it in the palm of his hand, his eyes locked on mine, while he strokes the red leather with long, firm fingers. My breath hitches. *Damn! Why does he affect me like this?* I wriggle in my seat, trying to reduce the tightness in my pants.

"Ashan, this is why I didn't come back. You know how I feel about you. That hasn't changed."

"I'm not gay," I hiss.

"That's what your mouth says. Your dilated eyes say something different."

"I can't, Michael."

"I know. That's why I stayed away." He grimaces. "I never stopped thinking about you."

My body throbs under his continued scrutiny.

"So, have you been with a woman yet, Ashan?"

"Of course, I have," I say. Too quickly. "Lots of women."

He smirks. "Did they make your blood surge? Your dick harden so painfully you thought you'd die if they didn't take you in their mouth and suck you dry?"

A tortured groan escapes my lips. His words are hard strokes along my dick, his continual caressing of the cricket ball like delicate flutters across my swollen balls.

"I'm not going to answer that. It's disrespectful."

"Mmm…"

"Michael, please…don't do this. Can't we go back to being friends? Like we used to be?"

"No."

My shoulders slump. What did I expect? I can't bear the thought of never seeing him again, but I can't give him what he wants.

"One kiss," he blurts out.

"What?"

"Give me one kiss. If you still prefer women and feel nothing for me, then I'll return to England and never bother you again."

Damn it. Why does he have to push?

He's as still as a leopard waiting for its prey to come closer. Only the slight shake of his hand gives him away.

I call his bluff. "Okay. One kiss. But not here."

He smirks. "Let's get going, then. I'll walk you home." He passes the ball to me, sparks zapping between us when his fingers graze mine.

We leave McDonalds, my heart pumping harder than a steam train chugging up the Kadugannawa pass as we walk side by side, not quite touching. He takes us on a detour through the park and stops when we arrive at a small alcove. It's a little hideaway we used to sit in when we were kids. It's still here. Untouched. Just like me. I lied before. I've tried kissing a few women over the years. It always ended with me gagging at the wetness of their lips or shying away from the softness of their breasts, their cloying perfume choking me.

He backs me up against a tree, his jet-black eyes never leaving mine. If it was anyone else, I'd be peeing my pants at the hard lines on his face. I hold the cricket ball to my chest as though it will protect me. He closes his hand over mine, holding me and the ball captive, and leans his face closer, his gaze dipping to my mouth. I squeeze my eyes shut.

His lips are warm. Firm. Mine part and his tongue sweeps in, plundering my mouth. It's like something snaps in my brain. I surrender to the blood surging through my body and pump my hips against his. It feels nothing like the women I've kissed. He's all muscle, his scent a spicy balm to my nerves. My dick throbs in my trousers, mirroring the pulsing of Michael's erection against me.

His erection! My eyes snap open. *What am I doing?*

Michael senses my panic and wrenches away, his face

flushed, eyes like a wild animal. He reaches his hand out towards me.

I flinch.

He hesitates for a second before tracing my lips with his finger. I stay still, my mind raw, my body flayed open.

"Why won't you admit it?" he asks.

"Admit what?"

"That you're gay."

"I'm not gay," I whisper, the words catching in my throat.

He glares at me. "Your body says you are."

"Michael, I'm…"

He growls, frustration rolling off him like smoke from a raging fire. "Don't! Don't fucking deny it. I'm sick of it."

I steal myself for the impact of him slamming me against the tree.

He stumbles away instead. "I never should have come back here."

"I'm sorry."

"I know," he sighs, his voice husky, the flames extinguished from his eyes.

We don't say anything more. We leave the small alcove, my innocence, while tainted, still intact.

Saturday morning arrives, and my father corners me before we leave the house.

"Today's a big day, putha. You need to lead the Colombo Cricket Club to victory."

"Don't worry, I will," I say, although the words feel hollow.

With Michael leading the Kandy team, I'm not sure we can win. I'm not sure I want to win. Guilt at hurting him, for not giving him what he wants, eats at my gut. Of course, I don't tell my father that.

"I know Michael is a formidable opponent, but you can win the game, Ashan. He's been away. He doesn't know the lay of the ground like you do. Use it to your advantage."

An hour later I stand on the pitch for the toss of the coin, the harsh sunlight blinding in its brilliance, but it does nothing to lighten the darkness encasing my heart. It's the first time I've seen Michael since he walked me home three days ago. There are crinkles around his eyes, charcoal rings underneath. I know I don't look any better. Sleep has been an elusive dream.

I win the toss and elect to bat. Michael gives me a wink, but it's a forlorn one. No spark. No cheek. Nothing.

My strategy plays out perfectly over the next two days and I feel a myriad of contrary emotions—relief, sadness, confusion—when the bails go flying at the end of the crease.

"Out!"

The batsman drops to his knees in despair. My team erupt in a flail of limbs reaching for the sky. We've won! My men rush onto the pitch like a flurry of ants, flinging themselves at each other and slapping the bowler on his back.

My Vice-Captain, Lakmal, is glowing as I embrace him. I let him go, my hands sliding down his arms. His muscles flex beneath my fingers, reminding me of the strength I'd felt when Michael caged me against the tree. Lust hits my groin like a lightning strike. I thump Lakmal on the back and jerk away from him. *What's wrong with me?*

Before I can dwell further, the team hoist me on their shoulders and carry me around the field. My gaze collides with Michael. He stands aloof, his eyes like milk chocolate swirls that have been left too long under the Ceylon sun. I'd shake his hand, captain to captain, if my men weren't carrying me away. Instead, I give him a nod. He nods back.

When we reach the dressing room, we're greeted to a raucous applause. My father's grin is a living thing all of its own as he hugs me.

"Well done, putha. Well done," he says, eyes shining with unshed tears.

"Thanks, Thatha. I'm relieved I didn't let you down."

"You could never do that."

He slaps me on the back and pushes me into the throng of well-wishers. I'm passed around like a newborn at a naming ceremony. Everyone wants to congratulate me, touch me, take a selfie with me: reserve graders, friends, family.

Eventually the fans fade away and we hit the showers to wash off the sweat and grime. I'm sitting on the bench putting on my shoes when red high heels come into view. My gaze travels over a long expanse of bronzed flesh that reaches all the way up to…I swallow and continue my upward exploration, the image of the woman's privates seared into my brain. She's wearing the shortest dress I've ever seen; her smooth breasts spilling out of the crimson red silk.

"Would the captain like a present for his win today?" she asks in a breathless voice, her gaze darting around the room, avoiding mine.

My body tenses. I've heard about this sort of thing, but I've never been on the receiving end before. Not this blatantly. But I'm the captain now. And our team has just won the competition. That means something. She takes my silence for a yes and drops to her knees, her small hands reaching between my legs. I grab those hands before they can make contact. She gapes at me. Confused. Behind her, Lakmal has dropped his towel and is standing naked, his erection jutting out like a welcome signpost.

I clear my throat. "Ah, thanks. But…" *Damn.* How to let her down gently without losing face. Lakmal's eyes are glittering with lust. He wouldn't say no.

"My men come first. They're the ones who really won the match. Can you give your gift to my Vice-Captain?" I point behind her to Lakmal. I'm sure he's more her type anyway. His unblemished skin (no ugly scars on him), little boy smile, and soft brown eyes have always made him a favourite with the ladies.

She twists her head, taking him in, in all his naked glory, then turns back to me, her eyes bright with anticipation. She likes what she saw.

"If that's what you want?" Her voice is eager, thighs quivering.

"Yeah, it is."

She gets off her knees and struts the few steps to Lakmal, her arse swaying.

Another arse comes to mind, and my dick twitches. *Maybe I made a mistake?*

Lakmal scoops her into his arms. *Nah.* It would have been humiliating for both me and her if I'd let her continue. This is better. I give Lakmal a thumbs up, pocket the winning ball and walk out.

The night air is quiet, the odd drunk weaving their way out of the ground. I'm too hyped up to return home yet. Club cricket is like a religion. So much rides on the outcome of these matches; our honour, our reputations, our masculinity. Which reminds me, as if I ever forgot, I never shook hands with Michael. That was rude of me. I walk towards the opposing team's locker room.

I stride through the door, the smell of defeat hanging in the air like a freshly slaughtered animal. Michael sits on the bench, head bowed. Alone. His upper body is bare, revealing the patchwork of tattoos covering his chest and abs which disappear down into his shorts.

"I'm sorry," I say.

He jerks his head up, his face a twisted mix of anger and despair. "You say sorry a lot, you know?" He scrubs his face and sighs. "Shouldn't you be celebrating?"

I squeeze the cricket ball in my pocket to give me courage. The leather is worn from the match, catching on the pads of my fingers.

"I wish there was some way we could have both won."

He stares at me like I've lost my mind and maybe I have.

"Cricket's all about one side winning and the other side losing, Ashan. Nobody wants a draw." His lips curl into a sneer.

"You were standing in for the Captain. It's not like you've been playing the entire season," I reply.

"True. But the Kandy team put a lot of faith in me, and I failed them. Losing sucks."

"We both know the winner was decided by the toss."

Michael leaps up and stalks towards me, his nostrils flaring.

"Why are you here, Ashan?" he demands, grabbing my shirt collar and shoving me against the wall.

I gasp at the daggers in his eyes as they bore into my soul. "I just want to make you feel better."

He's shaking, his forearms bulging. His hold on me is firm but not cruel. Even in anger, he's restraining himself.

That's when the truth hits me—I love this guy. I've always loved him. I've been wrong to deny it.

His hand wraps around my throat. "The only way you can make me feel better is if you get on your knees and suck my dick, like one of those little cricket whores has probably already done for you. And we both know you won't do that."

I've never seen him this angry before. It should piss me off or terrify me. Instead, my dick surges in my pants at the potent mix of lust and fury in his eyes. I shake my head. At least I try to. It's tricky when he's got hold of my throat.

"I didn't," I wheeze, sucking in air. "I offered her Lakmal instead."

He loosens his grip, and my knees give way. Strong arms shoot out and hold me steady.

"Why the fuck did you do that?" he asks.

"She's not who I wanted."

His eyes widen. He's wary and I can't blame him.

I swallow the nerves clawing up from my stomach. I've come this far. I know he wants me. I figure I might as well put it all out there. I drop to my knees in front of him, my face level with his crotch, and peer up at him.

"Let me suck your dick."

"Jesus, Ashan."

His hands come down to my head, but he doesn't push me away. Instead, he yanks me further into his crotch—his hard, throbbing crotch. The musky scent of arousal, his and mine, consumes me.

My hands dig into his arse.

He groans. "Fuck! After the other night I'd given up hoping you would ever feel this way."

I mouth his dick through his shorts, revelling in the way it jerks for me. He grabs my arms and hauls me up until we're standing face to face.

No. Surely, he's not going to say no? Not when I've finally accepted how I feel about him.

His eyes search mine. "Ashan, the last five years…not seeing you…not talking to you. It's been hell. If we do this, there's no going back."

I nod, my voice lost to his scorching gaze.

"The way I feel about you…I want a lot more than a quick fuck." He grazes my cheek with the back of his hand. "Are you sure?"

The darkness that has cloaked my heart lifts at the concern in his eyes, his voice, his gentle touch.

"Yeah, I'm sure," I say with a raspy voice. I press a chaste kiss on his lips. "Please be gentle. I've never done this with anyone. Man…or woman."

Michael shudders. "I don't deserve you, but there's no way I'm letting you go now."

He pushes me away from him so we're arms-length apart. His eyes gleam, his lips curling up into a playful grin.

"The winning captain is *always* the one who gets the blow job."

He drops to his knees, taking my shorts and underwear with him and winks at me.

"At least the first one."

Holy hell! My dick stands at attention, ready for action, like any good batsman. He grips it with one hand, peeling the foreskin back and dipping his tongue into the end of it to lick the pre-cum beading there. I throw my head back with a groan.

His tongue is stiff.

Wet.

Demanding.

I tremble, heat flashing through my body, and then he swallows me. All of me. My dick disappears into his mouth, his tongue flicking around the sensitive end before he works it further down his throat and sucks.

The suction! How the hell is he able to suck like that and not gag?

My dick is squeezed inside the warm, wet prison of his mouth and throat. I don't want it to ever end. My hips jerk and I fuck his mouth like a madman. He grunts from the impact of my balls slapping his face, but he never lets up and soon I'm shooting my load down his throat with a deafening bellow. He keeps sucking until I'm empty and then sucks some more before letting go with a pop. His gaze lifts to mine. He gives me a wicked smirk, licking my dick a few more times and cupping my balls.

He lets go of my sac and reaches down to the cricket ball that fell out of my pocket when my pants hit the ground. His eyes devour me as he stands, his face inching closer to mine. A whimper escapes my lips when he slides the leather around to my bare arse and slips it along the crack, parting my cheeks. My dick twitches at the contact, hardening again.

He nips on my ear and whispers, "Congratulations on your win, Captain."

Hours later, we're lying together on the side lines of the field. A few stray dogs are nearby. They ignore us, and we ignore them. I gently roll the cricket ball along the lines of a viper tattoo on Michael's stomach while he slides his fingers through my hair.

"I'm not getting engaged," I say.

His muscles tense, his fingers stopping mid-caress. "What will you tell your parents?"

I press myself closer to him and smile. "I'll tell them I'm already in love with someone."

Michael's throat muscles contract and a flush of heat rushes through me when I think about what that throat can do.

"How do you think they'll react?" he asks.

I sigh, "They won't be happy. They might disown me. But I don't care."

"Who?" he asks, his fingers digging into my scalp.

"Who, what?" I reply.

"Who do you love?"

I sink into the glowing ember gaze of my best friend. Now my lover. The man I nearly lost because I refused to be honest with myself.

"You," I whisper. "Only you."

Back in the Saddle Again

CORDELIA FOX

Lou Jones stood at the top of the hill; heart pounding, lungs heaving, leg muscles burning. She unclipped her pack and dropped it to the ground. The last three hours were a steady uphill climb, but it was worth it. Here was a view that most New Zealanders would never see in the flesh. Lou gazed out at the hills, stretching as far as the eye could see; the blue of Queen Charlotte Sound winking in the distance. She breathed in the smell of the bush. It filled her senses and left no room for the pain of the last year. She was strong now and at this very moment, victorious. The only shadow was the absence of her best friend Becky. She should have been here to share the experience. Instead there was Vincent, Becky's too handsome, too charming, too *everything,* cousin. Lou could hear him panting up the hill behind her. She pinned a smile on her face.

"You made it," she said.

Vincent gave her a grin, his perfect white teeth flashing in the sunshine. "Sorry to slow you down. I'm not as fit as I thought."

Hmm, thought Lou. He might look like he climbed hills for a hobby. His legs were muscled enough, but it was obviously just superficial. Typical man. All looks and no substance.

"Shall we have a break?" she asked. "We could brew up a cuppa and have a snack. The hut should only be a couple of hours away." She shouldn't be so mean. The poor guy was pale under his tan. He hadn't had the benefit of six months hill-training. No wonder he was struggling.

Stifling a sigh, Lou undid her pack to retrieve the camping stove. She couldn't believe her best friend was laid up in hospital with a broken leg, instead of out here with her. Walking this section of the Te Araroa track was their year's goal and then a hit-and-run driver ruined everything. Lou was all for postponing the trip until next summer, but Becky wouldn't stand for it. Walking the trail was a fitness goal for Becky, but for Lou it was a vital final step out of the bleakness that had almost pulled her under. Last week Becky magicked up her cousin Vincent, producing him triumphantly like pulling a rabbit from a hat. A man on the trip was the last thing Lou wanted, but Becky insisted he'd be the perfect walking companion. Finally, Lou agreed.

She watched Vincent swing his pack to the ground. She knew how heavy it was and it reminded her of women who insisted men were only good for one thing—heavy lifting. She'd joined the man-hating brigade. Faithless, cheating Tim had single-handedly ruined the whole gender for her. What a pity she couldn't transform herself into a lesbian, but unfortunately she just wasn't wired that way. Lou kept her gaze on Vincent, bent over, rummaging in his pack. No, her body was definitely hard-wired for men, despite her aversion to them. Lou turned resolutely back to the stove, but the image of Vincent's toned arms and shoulders conjured up a kaleidoscope of intimate scenarios. She swore softly under her breath. Her brain was behaving in all sorts of unwanted ways, not to mention her body. It was just her luck to be trapped on a hike with a man like this, when she'd sworn off men altogether.

"Is this what you want?" murmured a voice from behind her. Lou jumped. Vincent was standing close, holding out two mugs with coffee bags tucked inside. God, he was like a late-night radio announcer, with a deep sultry tone that flavoured his voice with something sinful.

"Yeah. Thanks," Lou muttered, feeling her face flaming red and her heart skittering in her chest. She knew what she wanted, at least what her treacherous body wanted, and it wasn't coffee. Lou was still wrestling with her torrid desires when Vincent's voice interrupted her.

"Smile," he called. Lou looked up to see him holding his phone, ready to take her photo. "For Becky," he said, shrugging in a way that conveyed unwillingness to defy his bossy cousin's demand for photos, and plenty of them.

Lou firmly shoved her salacious thoughts to one side and held out her hand for his phone. "I'll take one of you with the view in the background." She studied his image on the screen. A bit over six feet, at a guess, a lean, muscled body, topped with scruffy blond-brown hair. Becky said he'd been living in Australia for the last few years. He looked like a surfer, or maybe he was just a hippie. He'd some sort of knotted leather bracelet on his wrist. It caught her eye a few times, but Lou smothered her interest in it, just like she tried to stifle any interest in his body. What was the saying about the best-laid plans of mice and men? Lou sensed it would be more difficult than she expected to keep her mind Vincent-free.

"Can you somehow make me look less knackered than I feel?" Vincent asked, grinning into the camera. "Becky will never let me hear the end of it if I look exhausted in every shot."

"You look fine," said Lou briskly. Too fine. She wondered if it was possible for a person to spontaneously combust from unwanted lust. Goodness knows how she'd cope for another six days.

Vincent watched Lou. Her face was flushed pink from the exhilaration of winning. They'd played a wild game of Dutch. The hut was packed with an interesting mix of overseas visitors and locals; even some kids doing the track with their parents. Everyone was keen to learn a new card game and once Vincent taught them the basics, he sat back to watch the action. Lou's competitive side surfaced, and she'd played enthusiastically, one could even say aggressively; a fact that clearly made her ashamed now.

"Oh God," she muttered to Vincent. "I turn into an absolute bitch when I play cards."

He laughed. She was a stunner, this friend of Becky's. Tall and slim with long dark hair that his fingers were itching to release from the braid down her back. More than once today he'd imagined the cascade of dark silkiness over her naked shoulders and breasts. It was a fine way to pass the time, particularly when his muscles were burning on the never-ending hills. Her eyes were captivating too. They were an unusual shade, almost like whiskey. Intoxicating and addictive as strong liquor too, but despite his best efforts, he'd just caught glimpses of them. Lou spent most of the day with her face averted. Well, to be honest, most of the day she'd been well in front of him on the trail, particularly on those killer hills. It was only the sight of Lou's shapely bottom walking away from him that helped him up that last steep stretch. Now it was her rosy cheeks that were generating lewd scenes in his overheated brain. Flushed skin and groans of desire were all featuring highly. He forced his mind onto more appropriate channels.

"I certainly wouldn't have imagined that a caring, compassionate nurse would have such a mean streak," he said. "Those young kids are going to have nightmares." He laughed when he saw her appalled face. "Relax, I'm joking. You were a hoot."

Lou groaned. "Let's make an early start tomorrow so I don't have to face anyone."

Unable to help himself, Vincent reached over and took hold of the end of her braid. "Seriously, everyone thought you were great. Very entertaining, especially when you launched yourself across the table to grab the cards." He smirked at her embarrassed face, and then sobered up, staring at her braid in his hand. "There's nothing sexier than a woman with passion," he said softly, raising his eyes to hers.

Lou stiffened, holding herself still, and then abruptly stood up. "I'm off to clean my teeth," she announced and disappeared outside, without her toothbrush.

"Shit," Vincent swore under his breath. Stupid move. What an idiot. He was moving too fast, too soon. So what if he'd been smitten their very first meeting at Becky's bedside? He was clearly a poor second choice of companion, and he knew he needed to earn her affection. Blurted confessions weren't the way to do it. Becky warned him that Lou had gone through a tough time recently. The implication was that it was man trouble, and what had he done? Let his dick do the talking. And now he'd scared her away. Slow and steady, that needed to be his mantra. Vincent took a deep breath. He knew he was badly out of practice with women, but at least he had another six days to try to repair the damage.

Lou struggled awake, surfacing from the nightmare, panicked and disoriented in the unfamiliar space. She deliberately slowed her breathing, trying to calm herself. What had the dream been about? Horses. She'd been in a stable, assigned a never-ending job; something to do with bridles and saddles. She could still smell the leather and feel the weight of it in her hands. Vincent was there. He'd grinned in that lazy, sexy way he had, and opened another door to show her row upon row of leather horse equipment. She knew she had to put it all in order, but she'd never even met a horse before, let alone cared for one. Her dream-self was convinced she was doomed to fail. And then there'd been Becky's voice echoing through the dream: *You just have to get back in the saddle again.* It was just the sort of thing Becky always said to her: *if you get knocked off, you just need to climb right back on again.* It was terrible advice. If a horse threw you, you'd be mad to trust it again. Lou peered at her watch. It was 5.30am. She could hear the dawn chorus outside.

"Are you okay?" whispered Vincent. He was lying on the mattress next to her, staring at her in the half-light.

"Yeah, I'm fine. Just a strange dream."

No wonder she'd dreamed about him. He was practically in bed with her. Hopefully, tonight's hut would be a little less crowded and she wouldn't be crammed up next to him. She could feel the heat radiating from his body and her own temperature rose in response. Good grief, it was far too early in the morning to do battle with her lustful body, particularly when her brain was still full of dream-Vincent. She shut her eyes to block him out, but almost immediately felt him shifting closer.

"Tell me," he murmured. "I love hearing about other people's dreams. I can never remember my own."

Oh, this was unfair. His voice was even more sinful when it was pitched low and quiet. Lou felt her skin crawling with desire. She clenched her fists to keep them from reaching out for him and swallowed down her cravings. Doing her best to keep her voice steady, Lou whispered the dream to him, leaving out the part about Becky's advice. She was horribly aware her heart was racing, sparked by Vincent's proximity. He could probably feel it pounding, he was so close.

"That's spooky," Vincent said in a low tone. "I'm a saddler, well a part-time one. I make saddles and bridles for an equestrian company and pretty much anything out of leather the rest of the time."

Well, that explained the bracelet. He wasn't a hippy after all.

"I've got a leather-art exhibition in Wellington next week. Did Becky tell you?"

Lou shook her head. She'd been so infuriated at Becky's stubborn insistence she take Vincent on the trip she'd refused to listen to anything much at all. Maybe she'd absorbed the information unconsciously? How else would Vincent and his leather making skills make it into her dreams? Shit, now there was a whole other category of images to plague her mind. Vincent and leather. Vincent *in* leather. Sexy black leather.

"Lou," Vincent whispered. "I'm sorry for what I said last night." He hesitated. "It came out wrong. I didn't mean to make you uncomfortable."

"Forget it," muttered Lou. "It's no big deal." She rolled away and sat up, desperately needing to escape before she launched herself at him like she had at the cards last night. "I'm going outside to listen to the birds. I'll see you for breakfast."

"Crikey," said Lou, gazing at the river in front of her. She hadn't heard any rain during the night, but it had obviously been pouring further up the valley. She'd been in a hurry to leave this morning; mostly from a desire to put some physical distance between her and Vincent. Why hadn't she checked the weather at the hut where there was at least some patchy cell phone reception? Now she didn't know if the rivers would get even higher or subside in a few hours.

"Wow," whistled Vincent. "Wasn't this supposed to be a little creek?"

Lou pulled the map from her pack and pointed to their location. "The next hut is about 1km past here. I guess we need to decide whether we cross this or head back the way we came." She frowned, gazing around at the surroundings. "It's no good for camping here, but I suppose we could wait a few hours and see if it goes down."

Vincent looked at his watch. "Five hours walk back or half an hour onward. We'll still have enough daylight to make it back if you aren't keen to cross."

"I'm game if you are," she said, eyeing Vincent. The thought of backtracking wasn't appealing, especially since it'd be mostly uphill on the return trip. "Have you had much experience with river crossings?"

"None whatsoever," he replied with a grin, "but I'm happy to follow your lead."

Ten minutes later, after deciding on the best spot to cross and going over some basic instructions, they linked arms and started. The cold water swirled around them, higher and stronger as they moved steadily through the rapids. Suddenly, Lou stumbled into a deep patch. The water reached her waist and pulled her off her feet, but Vincent kept moving and dragged her up and out, into the shallows on the other side.

"Shit, that was deeper than I thought," said Lou, shivering, half from fright and half from the cold. Thank God Vincent kept hold of her. If it had been Becky at her side, they would have both ended up completely soaked.

"You should put some dry clothes on," said Vincent, his hands steadying her on the riverbank.

"No, I'd rather just get walking." Lou pulled away from Vincent and fastened her pack.

He eyed her uncertainly. "Are you sure? I can carry your wet clothes for you."

Lou shook her head impatiently. She hated being babied and just wanted to get to the hut. She'd wrenched an ankle when she stumbled in the river, not that she'd tell Vincent, and the sooner she could prop her foot up, the better.

"No, let's go. You go in front for a change. It shouldn't be far away." Lou clenched her jaw as pain snagged her ankle. She needed to toughen up. It was just a sprain.

"Good grief, Lou. Why didn't you tell me you'd hurt your ankle?"

Vincent wondered why she'd wanted him to take the lead when she was normally powering out in front. Her ankle was swollen and already discoloured. She must have been limping behind him where he couldn't see. He would have carried her to the hut if he'd known she was injured. Playing the hero might have even improved his chances with her.

"Don't fuss," Lou snapped. "Just dig out the first aid kit and I'll bandage it."

Vincent took a closer look at her. She was shivering, and her lips were pale. "Forget that. You're getting your clothes off, right now."

Lou looked up at him, startled, like a deer caught in the headlights. Vincent realised how his words must have sounded and felt his cock twitch into life. It wasn't a line he'd normally use to get a woman out of her clothes, but if using the threat of hypothermia got Lou naked, he'd go with it.

"I meant that you are obviously cold," he said calmly, ignoring the scurrilous voice in his head. "I think you need to warm up and then we'll deal with your ankle." He reached for her pack to find her some thermals. "Get changed while I get a fire started."

Ten minutes later the fire warmed the empty hut and Vincent heated soup to warm Lou from the inside. He sat behind her on the floor, in front of the fire, with his legs and arms reaching around from behind to envelop her.

"Just relax," he said as Lou stiffened. "You need my body heat. Drink the soup."

He breathed in relief as she complied and leaned back into him. She must have been much colder than she'd let on. Vincent wasn't terribly worried. He was sure she'd warm up soon, and she wasn't in any real danger of hypothermia. He, on the other hand, was in imminent danger of overheating. It was her smell that did it. She gave off an aromatic, heady scent that reminded him of his mother's spice rack, but unlike his mother's spice rack, it turned him on something terrible. He leaned a little closer to breathe her in, and his nose touched her braid. It was wet. That wouldn't be doing her any good. He tugged her hair tie off.

"What are you doing?" asked Lou, squirming around trying to see.

"Your hair is wet. It'll be making you colder. I'll dry it for you."

To his relief, Lou didn't protest. He carefully unbraided her hair, rubbing it gently with a towel and spreading it wide over her back. It was just as silky and lustrous as he'd imagined. It took all his effort to refrain from plunging his face into it. Vincent groaned softly. He'd have to move away from her, or she'd feel his cock poking into her back.

"What's wrong?" asked Lou.

"Nothing. I'm getting numb sitting here. Why don't you swivel round so your hair is in front of the fire and I'll have a look at your ankle?"

Hopefully dealing to her injury would deal with his hard on too. Slow and steady, slow and steady, Vincent repeated to himself. He grabbed the first aid kit and got onto his knees to lift Lou's ankle up. If anything, it looked worse in the firelight. He ran his hands gently over her foot, ankle and leg, unable to stop himself from touching her. Lou gave a soft gasp but didn't pull away. He ran his hands further up her calf. Her skin was silky and soft, just like her hair. God knows what her breasts would feel like. Vincent could feel the blood draining from his head, plummeting straight to his already engorged cock.

A flash of lightning, followed swiftly by a long rumble of thunder, cut short his fantasy. He raised his head, ready to count the gaps between lightning and thunder. He loved storms, and this one sounded really close.

"I think we got here just in time," said Lou. "I doubt

anyone else will turn up now. We'll have the place to ourselves."

"Yeah, it was a good call to cross the river, even if you're suffering for it now."

He reached for a bandage and, under Lou's instructions, made a reasonable job of stabilising her ankle. He'd just put her foot down when they heard the rain start. In moments it was thundering down, rendering conversation impossible under the hut's tin roof.

***

Lou gazed out at the pouring rain from the safety of the veranda. The frequent bolts of lightning gave glimpses of the valley and the thunder was loud enough to rumble in her bones. There was nothing better than a storm. Becky hated them, but Vincent was clearly a storm-lover like her. He'd cajoled her into getting into her sleeping bag for warmth, and then he'd carried her outside and sat her on his lap in a chair so they could watch the show.

Vincent's arms were looped around her, and the scent of rain mixed with his distinctive tang. Perhaps that's why she'd dreamt of him and saddles—he smelled like leather. It was a raw, manly scent, and it was as intoxicating as the storm. She could sit here forever, a warm man wrapped around her and a storm raging in front of her. Good grief, what was she thinking? She'd sworn off men, and for good reason.

"Do you like it?" said Vincent, his mouth so close to her ear she could feel his breath, warm on her cheek.

That was the problem, right there. She *did* like it, a lot, and despite the devastation Tim wreaked, she wanted more of it. Maybe it *was* time to get back in the saddle again? Lou swivelled her head, coming almost nose to nose with Vincent. She gazed at him, swallowed hard, and made her decision.

"Yes," she said. "I like it…and not just the storm."

Even in the half-light she could see Vincent's pupils dilating. So, she wasn't wrong. He was every bit as hungry for her as she was for him. Lou kept her gaze on him, waiting for him to make the first move. She didn't have to wait long. Vincent dipped his head and placed the softest, lightest kiss on her lips.

"Do you like this?" he asked in a low voice that made her toes curl. "Is this what you want?"

"Yes," Lou whispered.

She freed her arms from the sleeping bag and reached for him. This time there was nothing light about Vincent's kiss; it was pure heat. His taste filled her mouth, his tongue moving sensuously against hers and his hands tangling in her hair, holding her close. It was unbearably sexy, made even more so by the storm raging around them. Lou groaned helplessly, surrendering to desire. She twisted on his lap, trying to get closer. Vincent gave a low moan and she could feel his cock, hard beneath her legs. She was instantly wet and desperate to get out of the sleeping bag so she could wrap herself around him, but his mouth was on her neck and she abandoned herself to his assault.

"Vincent, oh God." Lou was incoherent with craving.

Vincent lifted his head and stared at her, breathing heavily. "I want you naked."

This time his voice wasn't just laced with sin, it was dark with demand and Lou's heart pounded in response. She reached for her thermal shirt, all too ready to meet his request, but Vincent's hands were there first. They were warm and gentle, sliding her shirt ever so slowly up her body, his thumbs dragging across her nipples. Lou shook her hair free and, as another bolt of lightning lit up the sky, she saw Vincent's face. The naked desire was so clear it made Lou feel powerful in a way she never experienced with Tim, or any of her other lovers. Vincent would do anything she wanted. She could feel it.

"Touch me," she said huskily, shivering slightly as the chill wind blew over her already hardened nipples.

Vincent placed his hands, almost reverently, on her breasts, gazing at her in hungry silence. Then he rolled her nipples between his fingers, tugging and pulling on them. Lou gasped as the sensation, part pain and part pleasure, shot straight between her legs, starting up a throbbing that demanded release. Dark heat flowed through her and she was frantic for more. She pushed the sleeping bag down over her hips, shimmying out of her thermal pants as she stood to face Vincent.

"More," she commanded, ignoring the pain in her ankle and her heart-felt renouncement of men. All she could feel was an overwhelming urgency for his hands on her body.

Vincent ran his hands up and down her legs, cupping her buttocks and lowering his head to her breasts. She swayed in response, leaning heavily into him and arching her back, loving the feel of his hot mouth, licking and sucking at her.

"Sit on me," Vincent rasped in between nibbles.

Lou climbed onto his lap, facing him, chest to chest, her legs spread wide on either side of his body. She leaned forward to claim his mouth, drinking in his taste and his heat. The power of the storm infected her with its reckless fury. She pulled at his shirt until it tore, until she had her hands on his naked chest.

"Lou," Vincent groaned, pulling his head back to stare at her. Then he reached a hand between her legs to touch her engorged, slick centre. "You are unbelievable…so luscious, so succulent."

He licked into her mouth as his fingers dipped in and out of her moistness. Lou was besieged by pleasure, spiralling ever stronger. She shook and moaned incoherently, the intensity rising higher and higher. Finally, she lost control. Bucking, and screaming, she came under Vincent's hands.

Vincent gazed down at Lou, lying in a limp, post-orgasmic stupor on the bed. He'd carried her inside after she crashed out on his chest, panting and shaking. He was still panting himself. He'd never been with a woman so passionate. It was like she'd channelled the storm. She was equally intense. The sight of her writhing and bucking in the lightning, her black hair streaming down, was profoundly erotic. The strength of his desire stunned Vincent. This was no schoolboy crush, it was overwhelming. He reached for her hair, stroking it gently. Lou rolled her head towards him and opened her eyes, still looking dazed.

"You are a goddess," he whispered. "A siren. A seductress." He smiled, loving her look of utter abandonment. "You are better than any fantasy I could come up with, and I've managed quite a few since I met you."

"Stop," Lou said, blushing and turning away.

"I'm serious," he said, running a hand over her body to cup a breast. "You are delicious."

He watched her face flush even pinker. God, he couldn't wait to fuck her. He'd place bets that the plunge into her hot silkiness would be mind-blowing, but first things first. Remember the mantra. Slow and steady. He leaned down and kissed her, tenderly at first, then nipping and biting at her lips. Vincent could feel her immediate response, her hands on his body, her hitching breath.

He pulled back to gaze into her eyes. "This time you are going to come under my mouth." He watched, absurdly pleased, as her pupils dilated, swamping the golden irises.

He worked his way slowly down her body, tasting and stroking every part of her, listening to her incoherent sighs. The way she responded to his touch made him feel like a sex-god *and* made him as hard as hell. It was a good thing there was plenty of room in his shorts. He'd be in real trouble if he was wearing jeans.

Lou's sex tasted as sweet as her mouth. As Vincent licked and nipped at her clitoris, he could hear her moans and protests, her fight to control herself. But it was her loss of control he wanted. He slid his fingers inside her, stroking and stretching as he licked and sucked harder at her nub. All too soon she was convulsing and shaking, screaming his name. Mission accomplished. He pulled up to feast his eyes on her again.

Lou surrendered herself to Vincent's gaze. Good God, she'd never known sex like this. So much for getting back on the horse. Her plan to seize control and grab some pleasure galloped right out of the paddock. The ride with this guy was out of this world. She thought back to her dream of saddles and bridles and all things leather. Of Vincent smiling sexily at her, just like he was doing now. She smiled back at him. Vincent was truly a saddle master.

The reality of the man was far better than any dream, with or without leather. And it wasn't over yet. They had the whole night to themselves, and perhaps tomorrow too, if the rain kept up.

Once she'd had a breather, she'd strip him off and ride him till he dropped.

Her man-hating days were over. She was back in the saddle again.

A Spark Amongst Stars

SAMANTHA MARSHALL

Sage Starburne stared at the elegant wooden interior of Everspark Booksmithery with equal parts hope and dread. Dark wood shelves lined the walls, their severity broken up by a comfortable sitting area complete with a steaming urn and a low table covered in sample books.

The shop was beautiful, one of many in the well-to-do part of Everspark Templecity, but none of those made his heart pump quite so hard in his chest or slick his palms with sweat. He'd expected to walk into a crowded room, but it seemed that with only ten minutes left before closing, even the shopkeeper found something better to do.

Nerves faded as Sage wandered the store, enchanted by everything he saw. A sweet, pale blue pocketbook for daily affirmations that made his blood bubble like champagne when he picked it up. A professional ledger that felt strong and austere, with tiger's eye set into the locking mechanism for protection. And a recipe tome with a cauldron tooled into the leather cover, the steam so lifelike Sage couldn't help but trace his fingers over it. And swore as he did that he recognised the smell of his mother's holiday stew cooking.

"May I help you?"

Reality rushed in with a snap and he took a hasty step back, hugging his portfolio to his chest. "I'm looking for Cascade Everspark."

The woman before him smiled, and Sage's world ignited. Hair so pale as to be almost white was bundled on top of her head in a messy bun, from which multiple strands escaped to curl lazily around her face. Glacier blue eyes sparkled in a pixie-shaped face that was all smooth skin and soft pink lips. Her frame was delicate but not without curves, clothed in a pink sweater and a sleek black skirt. Her shoes were a perfect match to the shade of her lips, which drew into a welcoming smile as she said, "I'm Cascade Everspark."

This was Cascade Everspark, owner of Everspark Booksmithery, accomplished spellcrafter and renowned grimoire artisan? Clearing his throat, Sage stepped forward and offered his hand.

"Sage Starburne."

"Lovely to meet you, Mr. Starburne." Cascade shook his hand, her smaller fingers warm and firm in his own. "Welcome to Everspark Booksmithery. Is there something I can help you with?"

"Yes—well, I hope so. I mean, perhaps we can help each other." Gods above, could he be more hopeless? Sage took a deep breath and shoved his portfolio towards her. "I'd like to show you something."

Acid coated the back of his throat at his own manner, but Cascade merely accepted the portfolio and turned to her desk to flip it open, leaving behind the faintest scent of...cookie dough? Great. As if she didn't already look good enough to eat.

"Oh," she breathed, spreading her hand over the first sample. "Oh."

"It's faux leather," Sage gushed, heart thudding as she rubbed the corner between thumb and forefinger. "Plant based, as sturdy as the real thing. No discernible difference in texture, more flexible to work with and simpler to colour."

Cascade flipped the green sample aside, smoothed her fingers over a soft mauve. "You made these."

"Yes." Hours upon hours of trial and error, swearing and sweat. "There's also a fabric similar in texture to linen, but it was the leather I thought you'd be most interested in."

Just that quickly, her face settled into professional lines. "Why is that, Mr. Starburne?"

"Please, call me Sage." He offered what he hoped was a charming smile. "I know how hard leather is to come by. Waiting for an animal to volunteer, paying commission to the Temple for your allotted metreage, no guarantee on quality—not to mention the amount of cleansing required. My plant-based leather has none of those restrictions or added costs."

Cascade tilted her head at him. "And you believe that I, a single, if reasonably well-known book smith, am the best person for this product?"

"Well..." Sage flushed, all his carefully prepared responses dissolving beneath the weight of her glacier blue gaze. "I tried several fashion houses, but they sneered down their noses. As did the saddler and the upholsterer. Then a friend told me about the work you do, the artistry and quality. As a singular business entity, you're restricted on how much leather you can acquire at any one given time. I thought—It seemed—Perhaps we—"

"It's true I'm heavily restricted with my leather access,"

Cascade agreed, flipping through the portfolio until she came to his price list. "Even though grimoires are an essential witch's tool, my smithy is seen as a luxury establishment."

"I'd be willing to sign a deal of exclusivity," Sage offered. When she froze, blinking up from beneath long, luscious lashes, he tried to ignore the rushing of his blood and waved a hand at the shop. "I'll also ensure the leather is perfectly tailored to receive your magic."

Cascade raised a snowy brow. "That would require us to work closely together. You'd be getting access to private spells and rituals I've never shared before."

"A deal of exclusivity," Sage repeated, squeezing his eyes shut. "And a confidentiality agreement. I'll even swear an oath."

Slender fingers touched the back of Sage's hand, shooting sparks of heat up his arm and into his chest. "It's not normally a great idea to sound desperate in a business meeting, Sage."

"I'm not a businessman." He offered a rueful smile. "Just a witch trying to support his family."

"You're married?"

"No, I care for my parents. My father was injured, and my mother couldn't run the restaurant by herself, so they had to close it. I—" Sage stopped and shook his head. "I'm sorry, this isn't relevant at all."

Cascade smiled, and it was all Sage could do to stay upright before the onslaught of sheer sensation it caused inside him. "It's all right. Did you work in the restaurant?"

"I was their sushi chef," he admitted, pressing his lips together in a thin line. "My magic is plant based."

"And when the restaurant closed, you found a way to turn your skills from seaweed wraps to plant-based leather." Cascade caressed the samples again. "Incredible."

Desperate, is what it was, but given he'd already embarrassed himself thoroughly, Sage kept that revelation to himself. "Thank you."

"You have a deal."

"I'm sorry?"

Cascade laughed, the sound filling the shop and sending his heart into a frenzy. "You have a deal. As soon as we sign the exclusivity contract and sort out an oath of confidentiality, you, Sage Starburne, are all mine."

Sage stared down at the petite hand she'd once again extended, a shiver rolling down his spine as they shook. "I've never wanted anything more."

***

Cascade frowned at the faux leather on her worktable as her spell leached out—again. The leather was a soft cream and would be perfect for a wedding album. But as with all the other samples Sage brought her over the last few weeks, her magic faded to nothing in less than ten minutes.

Growling under her breath, she tossed her tools aside and pressed the heels of her palms to her eye sockets. Deal or no deal, if they couldn't find a way to get the plant-based leather to hold her magic, she'd have to buy some actual leather very soon. A prospect that was unappealing on several levels; one, because it was far more expensive than Sage's leather. And two, because the man burned his candle at both ends—and several points in the middle—to find something that worked for her. If she needed to buy more leather, he'd be devastated.

Yeah, so her interest was more than professional. Who could blame a girl? The man was all three S's—smart, sweet, sexy. Just the right amount of tall, broad shoulders, dark golden skin, brown eyes and darker brown hair that no amount of product could tame. Every single thing about him made her heart beat overtime and delectable heat pool in her core. From the way he wore his jeans borderline tight to the tantalising few inches of tattoo she glimpsed when the neckline of his t-shirt shifted, she wanted more.

Cascade shoved upright as the sound of jangling keys announced someone at the inner door to her workshop. It swung open and Sage ambled in, casually dressed in worn jeans and a light grey knit, with a box in one arm and a large basket hanging over the other.

"Cass?" He stopped in his tracks. His brown eyes wide. "It's almost eleven at night. What are you doing here?"

"I finished my commissions and decided to spend some time working with your latest samples." Cass glanced at the clock and blushed. "That was about three hours ago."

"Lucky I bought extra donuts, then."

"Donuts?" Cascade grinned, weariness forgotten. "You bought donuts?"

Sage laughed, and she felt it in her bones. "Yeah, to keep me awake while I snuck these goodies in for you to discover tomorrow."

"Goodies!" Cass circled the bench, arms out for the basket he cradled in the crook of one elbow. "I love goodies."

The irascible man danced out of reach, eyes sparkling. "More or less than you love donuts?"

"More," she decided, reaching again. "Definitely more."

This time, Sage let her lift the basket from his arm, the brush of his skin against hers sending a tingle through Cascade's fingers. She risked a glance upward and found him watching her, brown eyes intense. "I'll bring goodies more often, then."

Gods above, that voice. Deep and thrumming, it hit her in all the right places, in all the right ways. Keeping her breathing even through sheer willpower, Cass shoved a pile of paper trimmings aside so she could set the basket down. It opened picnic style, revealing a long length of faux leather so deep a burgundy as to be almost black. She drew it out slowly, revelling in the smooth surface, the weight so like authentic leather as to be identical.

"Oh, Sage."

"I've been working on it all week, in my downtime." His voice was soft as he came to stand behind her, setting the box of donuts on a stack of boards that would one day turn into covers and spines. "The plant fibres are woven differently than anything I've tried so far, so I didn't want to bring it in until I was sure it was ready."

Cascade rubbed the leather against her face, sighed at the texture, the faint traces of Sage's scent—warm, buttery with a hint of spice. "It's so soft."

"Yeah, I noticed you prefer the softer leathers, so I focussed on that while I was weaving." He followed her to the cutting table, watched her slice off an eight-inch square. "I'm glad you like it."

"I love it." Cass laid the remainder on a pile of other leathers to her left, admiring the way his creation crinkled and curled into a nest just like genuine leather would. "Now to see what it can do."

Cass snapped her fingers and her grimoire appeared, a leather-bound tome in simple greys with a buckle closure. Pages flipped in accordance with her intent, settling on a spell for creativity and inspiration. Sage helped her set out yellow candles and sprinkle the leather with dried rosemary, then took half a step back.

"Over to you."

"All right." Cass touched the tip of her athame to the

surface of the leather. "Spirits and muses of the light, gift me with your blessed sight. Fill my head and let me be, a wealth of creativity. As I will, so mote it be!"

The yellow candles puffed out and the scent of rosemary filled the air as the herbs sank into the leather along with the magic. Cascade set her athame and grimoire aside and offered him a smile that was as tense as his expression.

"Now we wait ten minutes and see if it works. Want a donut?"

"Sure."

They ate in silence, staring at the clock as each minute ticked by. After the requisite ten, Cass cleared her throat. "Ready?"

"I guess." The poor man looked like he'd rather swallow his own athame, but he followed her back to the cutting table, nonetheless. "Give it to me straight."

Cass flattened her hand on the leather and gasped. "It worked."

"It worked?"

"Here." Cascade gathered the sample in her hands, feeling the soft brush of magic over her skin as she held it out. "See for yourself."

Instead of taking the piece, Sage closed his hands over hers, eyelids fluttering to half-mast as the ambience of the spell washed over him. "It really worked."

"Yup." Cass smiled up at his dazed expression. "Congratulations, Sage. You're the official and exclusive leather supplier for Everspark Booksmithery."

His lashes drifted all the way shut, his Adam's apple bobbing as he swallowed. "Thank the gods. I didn't think I was going to be able to wait much longer."

"Getting impatient to hold your first finished book?"

"No. Getting impatient to kiss you." Sage's eyes flicked open as he drew the scrap of leather from her suddenly nerveless fingers and tilted her head up. "I didn't want to taint the moment with malfunctioning leather and now...May I?"

Cascade's heart caught in her throat. Blood roared in her ears. Her world narrowed until there was only the soft touch of his fingertips, the heat of his body a hair's breadth from hers, the charged electricity in their shared gaze. "Yes."

Sage pressed closer, colour blooming on his cheeks as he lowered his head. Cass tangled her hands in his hair as their lips brushed, then settled together with sweet intent. She opened her mouth, and he took full advantage, sweeping his tongue inside to tangle with hers. He tasted of cinnamon and sugar and man, hot and wet with a hint of spice that was uniquely Sage.

"Cass," he gasped against her lips. "You have to understand, I don't do things like this lightly. If I...if we...it will be with all of me." He captured one of her hands and settled it over his heart. "I come with strings attached."

Something inside her squeezed and though her throat was thick, Cass dug for the words to match his courage. "I don't do things like this lightly, either...so I guess we're exchanging strings."

Sage's answer was a fierce, hot kiss, his strong hands tugging their bodies together until his thickening erection pressed into her abdomen. Cass slid her hands beneath his lightweight knit and a moment later it was gone, revealing a sculpted chest partially covered by an intricate knotwork tattoo. She traced her fingers over the pattern, and he shivered, catching his hands in the hem of her top and yanking it over her head. Her bra was practical but pretty, a deep red with hints of lace and silver thread. Sage growled in appreciation as he cupped her breasts. Then he bent to trail a line of nibbling kisses down her collarbone and into her cleavage, where he scraped his teeth over the swell of her skin.

Her knees gave out, but he was there, catching her as she fell and lowering her into softness. Cass laughed to find herself nestled in the pile of scraps, directly atop the burgundy leather Sage presented to her earlier. It was soft and warm against her skin, as soft and warm as the hands of the man who'd created it. A man who now knelt between her knees, the muscles of his abdomen rippling as he tugged off her shoes and socks and removed her jeans.

"Sage," Cass murmured, hooking her legs around his hips. "Touch me."

He crawled up her body an inch at a time, nipping and licking the length of her stomach, nuzzling her breasts, burying his face in her neck. "You. Are. Perfection."

She laughed, and he captured her lips, his mouth curved with a wicked grin she knew he'd have been too shy to share even a week ago. Delighted with the change between them, Cass ran her hands down his back to tease at the waistband of his jeans. She tickled his sensitive skin until they both gasped with laughter and he collapsed on top of her.

"Pants off," she whispered, nipping at his ear. "Right now. I want to see your magnificent body, Sage."

He blushed, drawing back to undo his jeans and hook his thumbs in the waistband. Looking up at her from beneath long, dark lashes, Sage slid the fabric down over his hips and her breath caught as she realised he wasn't wearing underwear.

"You like this?" Sage purred, pushing his jeans down one slow inch at a time. Cass sat up to help, and he stopped, shaking his head with a wicked grin. "Oh, no. You wanted to see."

His blush extended down his neck, but he didn't waver,

and after a moment's hesitation Cass returned to her reclining position on the pile of leather. "Yes, I want to see." She bit her lip, gave him a steady look. "Then I want to touch."

Sage swallowed and his muscles bunched, but he nodded, peeling his jeans down another couple of inches. Her breath came rapidly, her gaze locked on his pelvis as, ever so slowly, his cock eased free. It was thick, hard, and perfect, and she wanted it like she'd never wanted anything else in her life. When Sage stood to shimmy his jeans all the way down and kick them off, she couldn't help the choked whimper that slipped from her lips at the sight of him; tall, broad, muscular perfection.

Their eyes locked, and his gaze burned through her, a sweet blend of passion and embarrassment. Though the colour was adorable, Cass didn't want him to become so shy he ran—so she smoothed her hands up her own abdomen to knead at her breasts. She watched his mouth drop open in astonishment. While Sage stared, frozen, she unhooked her bra, slid it down her arms...and threw it at him.

The undergarment struck him in the face and Sage caught it on reflex, then burst out laughing, nervous tension draining away as he tossed the bra over his shoulder.

"Minx!"

"You know it," she murmured, slipping her fingers beneath the waistband of her panties. "Oh, Sage. I want you so very much. Don't you want to see for yourself?"

Sage's smile faded, gaze locking on her hand as he lowered himself to his knees. Before her fingers found their way completely south, he yanked her panties off, tilted her hips and buried his face between her thighs. She screamed at the first stroke of his tongue, legs wrapping instinctively around broad shoulders and her hands curling into his hair. The man might be shy, but he knew what he was doing, angling her pelvis this way and that while his fingers kneaded her butt and his tongue drove her wild. Just when she thought she couldn't possibly take any more, Sage shifted to a one-handed grip, slid a finger inside her, closed his mouth over her clit and sucked hard. Cass shattered with his name on her lips, her vision sparking and her body clenching over and over. He licked her through it, wringing every last pleasurable shudder from her limp body before he raised his head and met her gaze.

"Cascade Everspark," he rumbled, his voice tightening her body all over again. "May I make love to you?"

She wasn't sure she could speak, tried instead to pull him closer—but the infuriating man stood firm, eyes serious even though his body trembled with need. Cass swallowed, dug deep for her voice. "I think I might die if you don't."

"I need a yes," he murmured, smoothing his hands over her thighs and up towards her breasts. "I need to hear it loud and clear."

"Yes, Sage. I want you to make love to me."

His lips closed over her nipple at the same instant the broad head of his cock settled against her entrance. Thick and hot and so incredible she could barely think. Cass clutched at his shoulders, wriggling her hips to take him inside and he chuckled, releasing her breast to speak against her skin.

"Contraception?"

"I take a potion," she managed, "and I've got all my shots."

"Me too," he growled, and buried himself to the hilt.

It. Was. Everything.

Cascade clung to him, her mind reeling, her body

humming as they both took a moment to absorb the heady sensation of being joined. Then Sage groaned and shifted his weight, drawing almost completely out before sliding back in again. The incredible friction stole her breath, and she lifted her hips to meet his thrusts as they grew from tender and tentative to strong and sure. Magic crackled around them, sparking in the air and filling the room with the scent of cookies and warm spice.

"Cass," he rumbled, those gorgeous brown eyes dazed with passion. "Cass."

"Don't stop," she whispered, digging her fingers into his biceps. "I need you."

"I need you."

Sage kissed her, taking his full weight on one arm as he gripped her hips. Pleasure unlike anything she'd known flowed between them, intensifying with each deep stroke of his body inside hers. Cass scrabbled at his back, trying to bring him closer, faster, harder—and he complied, their rhythm shifting into a frenzy of passionate desperation. They shattered together, bodies shuddering and clenching in glorious release.

And Cascade knew, beyond a single doubt, that she was home. When Sage dropped his body onto hers, sweaty and spent, she cradled him close and blinked back tears. What they'd done was more than just making love; it was a sweet, sensual promise. One she intended to keep.

Sage withdrew from her body with utmost care and curled himself around her in their nest of leather scraps. Cass pillowed her head on his arm and snuggled into his chest, humming in delight while his strong arms held her close.

"Are you cold?" He asked, and yeah, there was that blush again.

Cass smiled up at him. "No. The heating spell on this place will keep us warm."

"Good." Sage cracked a yawn, his blush deepening. "Sorry."

"For what? It's well after midnight and you've been working like a demon." She kissed him, savouring the lingering taste of love and sweat on his skin. "Sleep."

Sage's brown eyes searched her face, and she wondered if her heart was as visible in her eyes as his was. When he smiled, she thought it might be, but rather than comment, he let his lashes drift shut and pulled her closer still.

"Night."

"Night." She closed her own eyes, revelling in the warmth that was Sage Starburne.

Sweet, smart, sexy. Hers.

Sage slipped through the door to Everspark Booksmithery in the early hours of the morning, an overnight bag slung over one shoulder. Locking the outer door behind him, he moved quietly through the shopfront and into the smith beyond. They'd piled the large workspace full of stock for today's launch; the first set of be-spelled journals covered in his faux leather. To make it happen, he and Cascade worked crazy hours for the last week, so exhausted by the day's end they'd been sleeping in the tiny loft she kept above the smith for emergencies.

Sage dragged himself one-handed up the ladder and found Cass waiting for him on the bed, her hair mussed from sleep and an azure satin robe around her shoulders. She'd a parcel in her lap, wrapped in black paper and tied with silver ribbon, and a gentle smile on her face.

"Clothes sorted?"

"Yeah." Sage dropped his bag on the floor by the end of the bed, ducking the exposed rafters of the ceiling. "I didn't wake you when I left?"

Cass shook her head, her smile turning naughty. "No, but I was ever so lonely while you were gone."

Sage's heart kicked up a notch, and he swallowed, still not quite able to comprehend the gorgeous, talented Cascade Everspark wanted someone as shy and bumbling as he. She patted the bed beside her, and he went, toeing off his shoes to crawl into position. Unable to resist the lure of her lips, he kissed her, groaning into her mouth when she opened it to sweep her tongue across his teeth. When he reached for her robe, however, she broke the kiss and swatted his hand away.

"Down, boy," she chided, eyes twinkling. "Stop distracting me when I've got a gift for you."

"I've got a gift for you," he growled, daring to waggle his brows even as he blushed.

Cass laughed, and it was worth it—then she set the wrapped present in front of him. "Here."

Curiosity bested embarrassment, and he dragged himself to sit cross-legged opposite her, giving the package an experimental shake. "A box of donuts?"

"Not if you're going to keep shaking it," Cass chuckled, poking him in the ribs. "Open it, already."

Her impatient streak was one of his favourite things, but on this occasion, Sage resisted the urge to tease her and instead tugged on the ribbon ends and tore into the paper beneath.

"Oh," he murmured, tipping the leather-bound tome into his hands.

It was a hefty thing, with pages edged in gold and a cover wrapped in burgundy leather. She'd tooled a knot-work border around the cover's edges, and his heart stuttered as he recognised the same knotwork that comprised his tattoo. 'Sage' curled across the centre of the cover in elegant script.

"What's this?"

"You don't recognise it?"

Sage set the book in his lap and ran his hands over the cover, blinking in surprise as lust spread through his body, heating his nerve endings, and setting his cock twitching in his jeans.

"This is my leather."

"Yes." Cascade's grin was wicked. "The leather you laid me down on when we made love the first time. Our...passion, our feelings, were indelibly set into the weave. If you hold it long enough, you'll get sounds and images, too."

He knew his eyes were wide and his mouth open, but Sage couldn't help it. Moreover, she was right; he could hear her gasps of delight, feel the incredible ecstasy of their joining. The moment he let the tome go, it stopped— but his erection was very much real and there to stay. Swallowing around the lump in his throat, he met her glacier blue gaze.

"It's wonderful."

"Thank you. I have no idea what you'll write in it, but that leather is the reason we're here, now, together." Colour flagged her cheeks. "I wanted you to have it."

"I'm not sure I'll even be able to write in it, with what it does to me," Sage chuckled. He eyed the book again, tracing a finger over his name. "There was more leather than this. Tell me you have a matching one."

"Of course; for all the times you leave my bed and I'm lonely."

"In that case, I better stick around," he rumbled,

setting the book aside. "I'd hate to be replaced by a book, even one as sexy as that."

When he tumbled Cass to the mattress she went, rolling with him until she came up straddling his hips, her robe falling open to reveal she was naked underneath.

"I thought the same thing. Make love to me, Sage?"

"Goddess, yes," he gasped, but she was already working at his jeans, shoving them down his hips just enough to drag his cock out.

A week ago, it would have made him blush, but he'd quickly learnt Cascade Everspark craved him with the same desperation he craved her. She wrapped a hand around his shaft, stroked once, then shifted and slid down onto him, drawing a groan from his lips.

"Cass."

"Sage," she teased, her voice a little breathless as she rocked him ever deeper. "My Sage. How I love you."

They both froze, her eyes wide with a shock that was surely mirrored in his own.

"Cass?"

"I…"

"Cascade Everspark, you own my heart." He stared deep into her eyes, gripped tight to her hips. "I love you."

"Good," she squeaked, and then laughed, the movement sending arcs of pleasure through his cock that had Sage gritting his teeth. Cass crushed her lips against his even as she moved in a sweet, torturous rhythm. "Good."

He could barely think, let alone speak, but Sage's eyes fell on the leather-bound tome she'd made. He reached for it, setting the ensorcelled book in the centre of his chest and dragging her body down on top of it. Sensation seeped into him, both from their bodies locked together and from the sensual vibrations set into the burgundy leather.

Cass whimpered, her body clenching around his, sparking a chain reaction that tipped them both over the edge. The book absorbed their ecstasy and cycled it back to them, taking Sage higher and higher even as it wrung his body dry. Cass sagged against the leather cover of the book, then laughed and pushed it to the opposite side of the bed.

"That thing is dangerous."

"I love it." Sage grinned up at her, framed her face in his hands. "I love you."

"My Sage, my lover, my love," she murmured, brushing hair back from his face. "I have just one question."

"What?"

Cass glanced at the bedside clock. "Do we have time to do that again?"

Sage laughed. His heart felt huge inside his chest. "Absolutely."

Blown Away

J A MACNALLY

In the middle of the packed exhibition space Ally stopped, entranced, a glass of red wine lifted towards her mouth. Impulsively she reached out but didn't dare touch the fragile glass sculpture in front of her. She was afraid even the merest contact might shatter its ethereal loveliness.

"Go on, it's okay to touch it," a gravelly male voice spoke behind her.

Ally turned, startled. The encouraging words sounded faintly suggestive, putting her immediately on guard. Her surprised glance travelled up, and up some more, to finally meet a pair of dark brown eyes in a well-lived face the colour and texture of leather. He smiled down at her, his expression welcoming. She noticed he was wearing black trousers with a leather belt, a black shirt under a brown leather vest and leather shoes, and thought, *Ugh*.

It was like looking at a male version of Liz the Lizard, which was how she always thought of her ex's new wife. She had a penchant for wearing leather mini-skirts, leather boots or heels, and always toting hideously expensive handbags.

Ally was tall, taller than most men, so having one look down at her was rare. She glanced again surreptitiously at his scuffed leather shoes, which had hardly any heels at all, so he really was that tall. She wore shoes with heels nowadays since she no longer had to pander to her ex's height-challenged ego.

"I shouldn't," she replied flatly, despite being sorely tempted, not liking the assessing way this leather-clad Lothario was regarding her.

She took another sip of her wine and willed herself not to succumb to the lure of exploring those smoothly polished glass surfaces. She'd always derived pleasure from exploring how things felt, not just how they looked. Her natural impulse was to touch whatever she found compelling, despite not always being able to follow through on her natural inclinations.

"No one is supposed to touch any of the displays. It says so there."

He glanced briefly at the nearby sign before returning the full force of his gaze onto her.

"Well, that's true as far as it goes. But as I made these…" his casual wave took in the nearby display of beautifully wrought, achingly delicate glass creations. "I'm okay with you taking a closer look. These sculptures need to be touched, not just looked at, to really be appreciated."

Having her own opinion about the value of tactile experience supported by this stranger made her look at him again more closely. She wondered if she'd misjudged him just because he liked to wear leather accessories.

He was not only taller than she was but also built broad and firm; a bear of a man, somewhere in his late forties, although his leathery complexion made it hard to tell. He'd probably worked outdoors in the sun for a large part of his life. His head was shaved bald, as smooth as the glass sculptures nearby, and she would have loved to run her hands over that polished expanse, despite not normally finding bald men attractive. He had a closely trimmed salt-and-pepper grey beard, and there was a gentleness in his expression that caused her to further reconsider her initial impression. It was just the leather he wore, reminding her of her ex's new wife's fondness for that material, which put her on edge.

"These are yours?" she asked, her surprise revealing her preconceived notion of what an artist working with glass would look like. It was a challenge reconciling his gruff, weathered exterior with these delicate creations. He looked more likely to have made the chunky, hard-edged blocks of smoky-coloured glass displayed nearby.

"Yeah, mine," he replied, making a sound, a deep rumbling noise she realised was laughter. "I know I don't look capable of creating something so fine with hands like these," and he waved his broad, blunt-tipped fingers at her playfully, "but there you go."

Ally blinked slowly, wondering if perhaps he was flirting with her, but why would he? And especially with her. She wasn't given to flirting, but she also didn't want him to think she was some empty-headed female just attending the exhibition to be seen in the right place. She was here to see a friend's sculptures, she reminded herself guiltily, but hadn't even tried looking for her yet.

Despite her discomfort, she found herself unable to move on so replied, "I imagine glass blowing is a lot more about dexterity and lung capacity, isn't it, rather than the size of your hands?"

She had a sudden, very distracting image of him running those capable, weathered hands over her bare skin, shaping her as he might a piece of molten glass. *Now where had that idea come from?* she wondered, blushing. She was divorced, a mother of two teenaged children, burned by her cheating ex-husband who had discarded her like a pair of old shoes before quickly trading up to a younger trophy wife. Ally acquired a layer of cynicism about men at the same time she lost her husband and her libido, so had no desire to ever let another man make a fool of her.

So why did she suddenly find this life-toughened giant so appealing and tempting? A vague thought of what her soft-skinned ex would say if he found out she'd had a fling with someone so roughly hewn tempted her to see where this conversation might lead.

Perhaps her long-repressed needs were waking up with a vengeance.

"Technique is important," he agreed gently in a slow drawl, moving slightly closer to her. She'd just taken another sip of wine and almost choked on it, wondering if they were still talking about glass sculpting. "But I like to think it's having an idea of what you want to create and being able to translate that into a finished product—that's what matters."

He smiled down at her again, extending his large hand towards her, and instinctively she grasped it. His skin was soft yet thick like leather, but in an appealingly masculine way. Had exposure alone to the intense heat of a kiln done this to him? She felt an immediate thrill course through her hand and up her arm at the intimate contact.

"I'm Sam," he said, "and I would very much like you to touch…my sculptures."

Sam was surprised when the woman suddenly released his hand and choked on her wine, then intriguingly blushed in embarrassment. He reached out and patted her back gently to help her overcome her coughing fit, amused by her reaction that revealed a lack of experience with flirting despite her age.

When she stopped coughing, she met his intent gaze, and he felt his interest sharpen. Her eyes were an unusual light green colour, not that dissimilar from the glass sculptures he created. He'd always had a weakness for green-eyed women. His ex-wife had green eyes, but they were narrow and assessing, not open and guileless like this woman's. Instinctively he knew this stranger would have little in common with the possessive woman he'd married, divorced and moved on from. Life was too short to harbour regrets or hold grudges; he much preferred to enjoy whatever pleasures he might encounter. This woman's soft fall of brown hair, large eyes and feminine curves promised quite a few pleasures for someone who hadn't been intimately involved with anyone for a while. But she needed to be handled with care because he sensed some wariness about her.

"I'm Ally," she replied when she could breathe properly again. "I—er—came here to see my friend's sculptures, but I haven't tracked her down yet. Are you a full-time glass blower?"

"On and off," he replied, his intent gaze examining her just a bit too closely for her liking. "I do it mainly for relaxation but it's getting to the point where I enjoy it far more than my normal work, which is in construction. I'm even turning a profit, although that's not why I do it. I have my own studio now, so I might do this full time in the future, maybe even hold classes for people."

She wondered if he would invite her to see his studio, and if that was his normal come-on line. Self-consciousness assailed her again. She feared the bright overhead lights bathing the various displayed sculptures were also highlighting the fine lines of crow's feet at the corners of her eyes, and the other tell-tale signs of her being past her prime.

Instinctively she stepped back, away from the lights, smiling awkwardly at Sam as she remarked, "It must be wonderful to do something you enjoy, to have that creative outlet. Well, I hope your display goes well. I must go track down my friend and see her display, too. It was nice to meet you," she ended lamely, unfailingly polite regardless of how she might really be feeling.

"Wait," he said impulsively and moved forward, fishing a business card out of his leather vest. He quickly wrote his mobile number on it before handing it to her. "If you ever decide you'd like to see more of my sculptures, or you're interested in having some lessons, please call me. I think you'd really enjoy the creative process, and I'd like to be the one to show you how to get started."

Ally couldn't decide if he just meant glass blowing or something more personal but tucked his card into her old leather wallet anyway before heading off to find her friend. She doubted she would ever see Sam again, but there was no harm in having this little memento of their encounter.

Ally hoped to avoid meeting her ex-husband Jeff again for a while, as he normally caught up with their two teenaged children each weekend without her direct involvement. She especially didn't want to see him with his new wife. She predictably carried an expensive leather bag by a top designer as though to advertise how much money her husband wasted bestowing costly gifts upon her. Even her leather stilettos matched the bag, which was tacky in Ally's opinion.

Despite that, Ally felt every one of her forty years as she stood looking at Liz the Lizard. She was your stereotypical blonde, blue-eyed nymphet with pert breasts and uniformly straight teeth that were dazzlingly white enough to cause snow blindness. Why did Ally's ex go shopping at the same plaza she'd chosen on impulse? She was terribly conscious of being dressed casually in jeans and a loose knit top. She wondered if Liz was always so overly done up, with impressively styled hair and excessive make-up. She almost pitied the younger woman if she felt this level of preparation was necessary to keep her older husband interested.

When Jeff spoke to her, she automatically ground her teeth, waiting for the latest veiled put-down.

"Ally, hello. You're looking a bit—ah—pale. Haven't you been well?" he remarked, and his new wife smiled, as though aware of looking her best.

"I'm fine, Jeff. Just doing the weekly shopping, you know, and all those things I need to fit in around work," Ally replied, wondering if her sarcasm would go over his head as it always had.

"It's great the way you still try to keep busy. I suppose working and looking after the kids doesn't leave much time for anything—or anyone—else, does it? I was saying to Liz just recently how much harder it must be the older you get, to find someone, I mean," Jeff remarked insensitively.

She felt a strong urge to wipe that insufferable smirk off his face. She was the same age as him, for crying out loud, so why should it be any harder for her to find someone than it had been for him? Perhaps she was still single because her expectations went beyond the superficial, or she was fussier, or Jeff had destroyed her desire for another relationship. She imagined hearing one day that Liz had left him in search of a more affluent man, which would be all he deserved after callously discarding his first wife like a pair of old boots.

Suddenly Ally remembered that hunky bear of a man, the glass blower.

"Who says I haven't found someone new?" she replied provocatively before she could stop herself. "There's a lot happening in my life now that you know nothing about. Well, I must keep going. See you around, Jeff, Liz."

She strode off before she could dig herself into a deeper hole.

<hr>

"Well, this is it, be it ever so humble," Sam announced as he pushed open the door to his studio. Ally nervously walked past him into the darkened interior, clutching her shoulder bag like a shield as her eyes darted everywhere.

She couldn't see much in the dimly lit space, but then he flicked on a switch and the room was flooded with bright light. A myriad collection of glass sculptures—large, small, delicate, robust, scattered or posed on every available surface—vied for her immediate attention. She was entranced, gasping in genuine delight. She moved forward to examine the delicate creations, her hand reaching out impulsively to caress a wave of aquamarine glass caught frozen with its crest breaking in white stylised foaming curls.

"That's one of my favourites. Funny you should go straight to it," Sam observed, appearing pleased by her genuine response, smiling as he leaned against the door frame. He wore a leather apron, so perhaps he'd been working before she arrived.

"It's so real, like a perfect moment in time," she murmured, running her fingers along its edge. She looked at him, her expression softened, unguarded, and he stood up straighter, no longer the casual observer.

"Like this moment, too," he said gently, moving closer towards her. "I'm really pleased you decided to call me about seeing more of my work and perhaps having lessons. I was hoping you would."

"Um, about that. I should confess I did it on impulse, as a way of getting back at my worthless ex-husband. He'd the gall to imply that unlike *him*, I would find it hard to attract someone given my age. So, I'm not sure if I'm here for lessons or to find out whether I imagined the…connection…between us at the exhibition last week."

She was instantly appalled to have made such a revealing admission and felt heat rise in her cheeks.

"There was definitely a connection. I'm happy to give you lessons in glass blowing or anything else you have in mind. Just say the word." He paused before adding cheekily, "I'm also wondering if there's any chance you might run your fingers over me like that."

She stilled her hand on the sculpture and laughed in surprise, saying doubtfully, "I'm not sure if you're joking, just flirting or…"

"I mean it. Ever since I saw you at the exhibition… there's something about you that really appealed to me, got my creative juices flowing. I hope this doesn't sound too full on so soon, but all I can think about is exploring every single inch of your body and recreating you in a sculpture. That, and a lot more."

She blushed harder, looking away in embarrassment, even as a small part of her delighted in being the recipient of his attention. But maybe he did this with any lonely, past-her-prime female, she thought sadly, seeing her and a long line of others as easy sexual conquests.

"That does seem rather full on. I find it hard to believe that you'd see someone like me being that attractive, especially on such short acquaintance," she replied, almost challenging him.

Even as she replied, she wondered why she wanted to discourage him. So what if he did this with lots of other women? It had been years since she'd had sex with a man, and much longer since it had been passionate, orgasmic sex, which she imagined it would be with Sam. If he were genuine or just a glass-blowing Casanova, what did it matter?

"What do you mean, someone like you?" he asked, puzzled, a frown breaking up his face so that his weathered skin wrinkled, reinforcing the differences in their ages and experiences.

"A divorced mother of two teenaged children, with stretch marks, crow's feet, breasts no longer perky—you get the idea." She listed her foremost flaws, aware this was how she thought of herself nowadays: wasted, used up, no longer a desirable woman capable of inspiring lust or love in someone else.

He smiled, moving closer, his hands cupping her face, his fingers softly tracing her cheekbones.

"In case you hadn't noticed, I'm no spring chicken myself. Yes, you are a mother, which is something I admire immensely after my ex refused to have children because she said they'd ruin her figure. Any stretch marks you might have are a badge of honour, and your children are proof you're someone capable of nurturing others. That means a lot more to me than perky breasts. Yours look fine from where I'm standing by the way. I'm attracted to you because you're real, you have experience, your own opinions, and I find all that a real turn on. I also think you're incredibly attractive."

"Is this where I say something like *you had me at hello?*" she murmured, smiling gently to show him she was joking.

Inside she was becoming a throbbing jumble of arousal, anticipation, and terror, just because he was touching her so gently. Could she really go through with this—have sex with someone she had only briefly met a week ago? His declaration didn't allay her self-consciousness about her imperfect body. Yet despite her trepidation, she was also aware of an undercurrent of excitement at the prospect of having uninhibited sex with this incredibly virile looking man.

"Definitely," he concurred, smiling back.

She raised her hand to touch his face in turn, marvelling at how smooth his skin was, like beautiful, expensive leather. She'd a sudden image of him naked, aroused, his body molded all along the length of hers, and she sucked in a nervous breath.

"I admit I gave you my card on the pretext of coming here for a glass blowing lesson, or to see more of my work. But since you've also admitted you had other reasons for being here, will you let me show you how much I want you? I can tell you don't believe me, so let me prove how desirable you are to me. Let me explore you, trace all your curves, find where you're most sensitive, learn your secrets. Then I'd like to recreate that experience in a glass sculpture if you'd let me."

As Sam spoke almost hypnotically, he gently swayed closer against her. His eyes were intent on hers as his hands dropped from her face to her shoulders, gripping them lovingly before moving to touch her back. He slowly traced the outline of her rounded hips, and then her tightening buttocks that clenched in reaction. When his hands fleetingly reached lower to caress the backs of her thighs, she thought she might come right then. *Oh, God, that feels incredible*, she thought. He was as gentle and reverent with her as he would be exploring a glass sculpture, and she felt incredibly treasured and precious, safe with him.

"Would you like me to keep going?" he asked, his voice even gruffer than usual.

"I think so. Just understand that I've never done anything like this before. It's so out of character but being a dutiful wife didn't get me very far, so I'm willing to take a chance on doing something impulsive for a change. Does that sound bad, like I'm using you to prove a point?" she replied, her cheeks flushed and her breath hitching in anticipation.

"I don't think you'd do this with just anyone. There's a definite connection here. I felt it, too, and I'd like to see where this takes us. I don't normally come on to strange women, you know; I'm too busy working or making my sculptures. And I've never invited anyone to my studio before, but I'm going to go with my gut and see where this takes us, if you'll trust me?"

"I do trust you, which is strange, so if you're okay with this, whatever it is, I am, too. So yes, please keep going."

"Well, since you've asked so nicely," he whispered, as his mouth lowered gently to touch hers. He fitted his lips to their shape, lingering there forever it seemed, making her feel like she'd never really been kissed before.

Her lips eagerly returned the pressure of his, seeking to

learn his taste, his shape, his smell, becoming drunk on his proximity. Her heart raced, her nipples tightened, and her insides throbbed with sensual need.

Their kisses deepened, grew more demanding, their mouths opening against each other as their tongues met, tangled, explored, retreated and returned, parrying like fencing opponents seeking an advantage. He growled deep in his throat and his hands tightened around her, drawing her closer against his taut, heat-hardened body, while she pressed against him, as close as their clothing allowed. They staggered blindly back into the far corner of the studio where there was a padded bench, probably just used for contemplating his sculptures, drinking a coffee, or eating a quick meal. But now it was destined to serve a more intimate need.

Ally vaguely realised she'd fallen backwards onto a couch or something similar. But her focus was purely on the man who landed beside her, their mouths seeking each other's again to resume their passionate embrace. She wasn't sure who removed their clothes first. Whether in those initial moments of passion they removed each other's clothing instinctively, stripping each layer, each item away, and assisting with a shrug or a wriggle to remove the obstructing garment. It was dimly lit here, and her former inhibitions about revealing her body receded as her need for this man, for this experience, erased her shyness, replacing such irrelevance with what really mattered.

She felt his bare chest under her exploring hands and uttered an inarticulate sound of pleasure, surprised to discover how warm and firm he was. His leathery skin was softer here, and she wanted so much to breathe in his scent and taste him. A primitive need was taking over rational thought as sensual impulses pushed aside her civilised veneer to strip bare the female beneath. She hungered to know this man as intimately as she might have stroked one of his sculptures, to experience the aching pleasure of mutual physical release. Impulsively she stroked his shaved head, enjoying its sleek smoothness, and imagined it between her thighs as he tongued her. Oh, if only he did that, she would die a happy woman.

Sam peeled off her top and made quick work of removing her bra, freeing the full, flushed breasts that he held gently in his calloused hands. He groaned when her mouth sucked on his nipples, nipping at them playfully before seeking to taste other parts of his body with her exploring mouth. He suckled on her breasts as well. His hands cupped them together while he drew each nipple into his hot mouth, lathing them one after the other repeatedly so she writhed and moaned against him encouragingly.

When the throbbing in her body became too insistent, she sought the zipper of his jeans. She pulled it down impatiently, eager to find his rigid length and caress it, while breathlessly imagining that hot cock plunging inside her.

He chuckled against her, saying, "Easy, Ally, don't damage the goods."

"Sorry," she whispered, then freed him, and he wriggled fully out of his jeans and briefs, before quickly divesting her of her remaining clothes.

He ran his hands appreciatively up and down the length of her legs. His growl assured her he found nothing wanting.

Ally gripped his erection in her small hand, aroused by how large and thick it was—a fitting size to match this bear of a man. She rubbed her hand up and down his length, squeezing and kneading the hard core beneath the softer outer skin. She gently touched the moisture at the tip, then spread it over his length with her fingertips.

She'd forgotten how much pleasure there could be in such intimacy, in bringing a man closer and closer to the brink of ecstasy with sensual caresses. It was a powerful, heady sensation, and she gripped his length more firmly, loving the unrestrained sound of his gasps, his unsteady breath, and the musky scent of his arousal.

She imagined how he would feel inside her, filling her, plunging into her repeatedly until she came and came again, and the thought made her feel deliciously wicked.

***

Sam was equally entranced by Ally's body, by her soft curves, her full breasts and the little dips at hips, elbows, and knees. He was already imagining a series of sculptures inspired by her body, which made him smile in anticipation. While she caressed his taut erection, his hands wandered down her smooth legs, beyond her thighs, before discovering she was ticklish behind her knees.

One hand travelled upwards again to find her moist, hidden opening. Slipping a finger inside her wetness to test her readiness, he loved the way she moaned, and how she stretched closer against him, inviting him to do more. He removed his finger and then slipped two back inside, pleased by how tightly her muscles gripped him. How wet and ready she was as he plunged his fingers inside her, seeking her most responsive spot.

She continued to caress his erection, her fingers instinctively finding the exact spot where he was most sensitive, too, and he groaned appreciatively.

Sam removed his fingers eventually and gently shifted their bodies until she was fully under him. He nuzzled her breasts once more, paying homage to their round fullness and tight buds with repeated, assiduous suckling that made her pant and groan in mounting arousal. He blew gently on the moist tips, as though cooling one of his sculptures, and she smiled at him in appreciation.

The blunt head of his erection butted against her thighs, and then slipped unerringly towards her waiting entrance, rubbing erotically against her mound until it found the engorged lips. Her thighs parted wider encouragingly, and his cock slid fully into her body, making him rumble with pleasure as she tightened around him. She was so tight yet slick that he kept withdrawing and then plunging back inside her again, the force of his body against hers driving him deeply inside her, making her shudder in pleasurable response.

The pleasure must have grown too much because she writhed beneath him. Her rounded hips lifted instinctively to meet each thrust, welcoming him inside her every time, her legs hooking behind his back so he could drive deeper inside her. The fullness of him pounded against her clit. Combined with the deep penetrations of his thick cock inside her, it compelled her to cry out when her orgasm hit her full on like a truck at high speed.

When he felt her muscles contracting convulsively around his cock, he knew she was coming, and it unleashed something untamed in him. His body surged like a piston in and out of her tirelessly, their sweat-drenched skin slick and sliding in easy rhythm. He felt his orgasm overtake him, stiffening his muscles as his cock spasmed in release, filling her, and permeating the air around them with the scent of their coupling.

Still, he convulsively emptied himself within her, compelled by her cries and the power of her muscles' contractions to surge into her repeatedly, so she came again, crying in surprise as she gripped his arms.

Eventually he eased out of her gently to lie close beside her, their lungs drawing in air. He groped nearby and found an old t-shirt, which he offered to her so she could wipe away some of the results of their passionate encounter.

She turned her head slightly to gaze at him, saying softly, "I can't wait to see what you create based on this."

He couldn't even draw in enough breath to reply, just managing a raspy laugh, aware when she put her hand in his. He gripped it in response as they fell into an exhausted yet happily sated sleep.

At the following year's exhibition, Sam's glass sculptures were more abstract, still delicate but intriguingly suggesting intimate aspects of the female anatomy. He laughingly dismissed this conjecture when queried by buyers, even as his eyes sought out those of the green-eyed woman wearing his favourite leather vest, who stood a respectful distance away.

Sam's sculptures were arranged on lengths of polished driftwood, and the combination of the natural material supporting the delicately curved glass shapes compelled each person who stopped by the display to touch them.

Sam didn't offer his business card to people for lessons at his studio. He had the only person he needed or wanted right here.

Ally watched Sam proudly as he spoke with people, his manner friendly yet respectful, while she idly considered some ideas for sculptures she was planning now she'd learned the basics of glass blowing.

Perhaps delicate little glass handbags and boots, or maybe lizards.

As long as there were lots of tactile things to touch and explore, including Sam, she would be happy.

Leather-bound

NOVALEE SWAN

Alyssa Elliot knocked on the imposing door of the Mayfair mansion, trembling like a wet kitten. Taking a shortcut through Hyde Park was a mistake. When the heavens opened, she'd been caught without shelter. Her shearling coat was soaked through to her white oxford shirt, and her navy pencil skirt was clinging uncomfortably to her nylons.

Fortunately, it didn't matter.

The only thing that needed to stay dry was safely ensconced in the insulated, airtight, and—most importantly today—waterproof briefcase she carried. Still, Alyssa hugged it to her body like a mother protecting her child.

She knocked and pressed the doorbell again and double-checked her wristwatch.

She was on time.

Maybe the chime of the bell was drowned out by the driving rain.

She bit her lip, unsure how to proceed.

Water dripped uncomfortably down her neck and wet hair clung to her scalp. An ear-splitting crack of thunder made her jump, and Alyssa crowded closer to the large wooden door. She wasn't afraid of storms, but today it seemed like the gods were venting their anger on the earth.

She was about to fish for her phone in her coat pocket when the heavy door swung open. Before she could speak, a hand emerged and wrapped around her wrist, tugging her over the threshold.

Alyssa stumbled forward into the tall frame of Sai Dewan.

The briefcase was a buffer between them, but her forearms were pressed against his strong chest and his hands bracketed her shoulders. Alyssa looked up into his dark brown eyes and reacted the way she always did when she saw him—multiplied by one thousand since they'd never made physical contact. Her arms tightened around the briefcase.

"Miss Elliot." His voice held traces of his Indian heritage.

"Mr Dewan." The words emerged huskily, and she cleared her throat.

"Are you all right?" he asked.

She nodded…and began trembling again.

"You're cold."

The hands at her shoulders dropped. One claimed the briefcase from her, and the other grasped her hand. Then he turned and began leading her along the long, black and white tiled hallway, past a grand staircase. Alyssa barely registered the décor—just a sense of understated wealth. The sensation of Sai Dewan holding her hand befuddled her. She trailed behind him, unresisting.

He led her through a set of wide double doors into a large library, then off to one side, to an open fireplace. Sai didn't stop until he'd positioned her in front of the warm flames. He set the briefcase down and exited the room without a word.

Alyssa was left unsure…was she supposed to wait? She turned, surveying the room, and immediately forgot the discomfort of her wet clothes.

As might be expected of a home in one of the oldest and most exclusive suburbs of London, the library was reminiscent of a Regency fantasy. Floor to ceiling bookcases lined three walls, with thousands of leather-bound volumes. On the mantle above the hearth was an antique Georgian clock with a silver dial. Opposite the doorway, beyond a large walnut desk, was a picture window covered by heavy velvet drapes in midnight green. They were drawn, but she could hear the pitter-patter of rain against glass. Positioned in front of the hearth was a brown leather chesterfield sofa, and an open book lay down-turned to one side. A crystal tumbler with amber liquid rested on an ebony end table, next to a banker's lamp. A matching lamp illumined the surface of the walnut desk in an intimate golden pool. The only other light came from the flickering flames of the fire.

Alyssa couldn't resist walking to the nearest bookcase and running her fingertips down the hard leather spine of one book. Divina Commedia. Her fingers moved on to the next, Evelina, and she smiled softly as she perused the titles.

He had good taste.

"Why aren't you in front of the fire?"

Alyssa started when she heard Sai behind her, spinning quickly, as though she was in the wrong. He stood framed in the doorway, in faded jeans and a soft, black jersey sweater. He held a pile of towels and a long robe in a deep, dark green, like the drapes.

She shivered, suddenly feeling cold again.

Alyssa walked back to the fireplace as Sai approached from the doorway. They arrived at the same time. He dropped the robe onto the leather chesterfield and handed her a fluffy white towel.

Alyssa took it, wiping her face and neck. Then she wrapped the towel around her long ponytail, blotting out the water.

"Take off your coat."

At those words, Alyssa's eyes slid unwillingly to Sai. His brown skin looked golden in the firelight. Light reflected off round spectacles. She'd never seen him in them before. Her eyes strayed to the open book on the sofa. He'd been reading. That wasn't surprising. Sai Dewan was a collector of rare books. Not the kind who collected for show—she knew plenty of those—the kind who saw books the way she did…as priceless treasures.

It made Alyssa recall her reason for being there—and her reasons for not wanting to stay longer than necessary. Removing her coat seemed like the first step towards a line she should not cross.

"It's just a little damp," she said quietly.

"You're dripping on my carpet."

Alyssa looked down automatically, but she couldn't detect any water droplets on the botanical pattern of the red and gold Mughal carpet. She wondered if his company made the gorgeous floor covering. She'd heard the Dewans were an old name in textiles.

Distracted, she was unprepared when Sai came close. She looked up…and up since he didn't stop until he was inside her space. Her tortoiseshell eyes widened. Alyssa was small, so he was a good nine or ten inches taller. She dropped the towel when his hands went to the large enamel buttons on her coat. Before she could protest, he'd undone them and was stripping the wet wool off her shoulders.

Alyssa stared up at him, disconcerted. Once the coat was gone, his dark eyes dropped to her chest, and she heard his indrawn breath. His gaze lingered for a moment before he redirected it in a deliberate way that made Alyssa look down and instantly cross her arms. Her lace bra was visible through her wet shirt.

Sai picked up the robe from the chesterfield and handed it to her. "Take off your clothes and I'll dry them." Without another word, he left the library.

Alyssa stared after him, holding the robe. If taking off her coat was the first step towards a line she shouldn't cross, this was steps two through nine. She looked help-lessly around the room. But what other option was there?

She closed her eyes, gritted her teeth and took a deep breath. Then she peeled off the cold, clammy clothing with difficulty, until she was left in only her underwear. She weighed the option of leaving her bra and panties in place, against the wet patches they'd make on the robe. Worried Sai would return while she dithered, she quickly stripped them off and balled them up inside her navy skirt.

She used a fresh towel to dry herself then slipped on the robe, belting it tightly. Its folds enveloped her in dry warmth and fabric soft as mink. She caught the scent of Old Spice. Then she sat on the chesterfield and pulled the silver barrette from her low ponytail, releasing the long caramel strands, dark with water. She began drying her hair in front of the fire.

There was a knock at the door.

"Come in," she called softly. It felt strange to be giving Sai Dewan permission to enter his own library. That was probably the reason she didn't turn to look at him, just stared at the flames as she worked the towel through her hair.

Without a word, Sai gathered her wet clothes and left the room again. As Alyssa waited, she couldn't help remembering the first time she'd seen him, at an auction at Sotheby's. He'd outbid her on a first edition of The Vicar of Wakefield.

They hadn't spoken a word, but a week later, that book arrived at the British Library, addressed to her, with an offer for a long-term loan to display it in the rare books collection. Alyssa never expected that less than twelve months later she'd be sitting in Sai Dewan's library, wearing his robe.

This time when he returned, he didn't knock.

He crossed to the chesterfield and held out a cup of tea. Alyssa dropped the towel into her lap and accepted it gratefully. She raised the teacup to her lips, inhaling the scent of cardamom and chai. The hot liquid diffused warmth throughout her body.

"Thank you," she murmured.

"You're welcome."

He was always courteous, in his speech and his actions. She'd noticed that when they met, soon after the auction, at a gala at The London Library. They hadn't exchanged more than a few words before Alyssa escaped for the evening, as had become her habit whenever she encountered him. It was something that seemed to occur regularly in London's art circles since that day. But that respectful solicitude, in a man as equally cultivated as he was masculine, was dangerously attractive.

A flash of lightning bled around the curtains and a heartbeat later, thunder rattled the windows. The storm settled overhead.

She shouldn't linger.

Alyssa reached for the briefcase, but Sai was there first. "Drink your tea. I'll do it. Unless you have any objections?"

None came to mind, so she nodded slowly.

Sai carried the briefcase across the room and placed it on the walnut surface of the desk. He flicked the clips open. Then he removed a leatherbound copy of La Princesse de Clèves.

Alyssa rested against the arm of the chesterfield, half facing the fire, half facing Sai. She sipped her tea, covertly studying his handsome face, lashes lowered.

He placed the volume into a book cradle in the middle of the desk and set the briefcase on the floor. Then he examined the cover, where a beautiful geometric pattern was embossed into the leather. He opened the two intricate gold clasps securing it and began to carefully turn the vellum leaves.

After a few minutes, he looked up. "Your work is excellent."

"Thank you," she murmured.

La Princesse was in poor condition, but Alyssa stabilised the volume, repaired the insect damage and secured the binding—all with an invisible touch, so the book looked unaltered.

"I have another commission for you."

Alyssa's interest piqued. She rarely accepted freelance work outside her job as a conservator for the British Library. But Sai could afford the rarest of the rare—works far too tempting to refuse, despite her unwise attraction to him. That's why she'd been unable to resist when he'd sought her out for this commission.

Sai unlocked a climate-controlled section of bookcase and deposited *La Princesse* inside. He removed another book and set it on the desk. Alyssa placed her empty cup on the end table, next to the crystal tumbler, and approached this new treasure. The long robe brushed the floor as she walked.

Sai shifted to make room for her.

Entranced, Alyssa forgot to maintain her customary distance from him. A soft smile spread across her lips as she surveyed the red morocco clamshell case. There was a Cosway-style miniature embedded in the centre, an erotic scene.

Her head tilted curiously, and she opened the case to find a matching volume inside. The red leather was vibrant, inlaid with a gilt border and cornices. Another erotic miniature graced the cover. Alyssa lifted the volume free of the case, catching sight of the heavily gilded spine and the title.

The Kama Sutra.

Alyssa gently placed the book into the cradle on Sai's desk and set the case safely aside. She wanted to examine the miniature in more detail, but she was too conscious of the man standing beside her. She opened the cover. There was some spotting on the title page, but in red and black ink it read: The Kama Sutra of Vatsyayana. Translated from the Sanskrit. In Seven Parts, with Preface, Introduction, and Concluding Remarks. Benares: Printed for the Hindu Kama Shastra Society. 1883. For Private Circulation Only.

Alyssa's eyes flicked over to Sai. "This is a Burton first edition." Richard Burton commissioned a translation of the ancient Sanskrit text. He'd then created a fake publishing house to print it for private circulation so he could circumvent laws that prohibited the public circulation of works considered 'obscene'.

"Mm," Sai confirmed softly. "Orientalism at its finest."

Alyssa understood his meaning. The translation was

problematic, and unfaithful to the original. "Why did you acquire it?" Given his heritage, she expected he was more aware of the issues that accompanied Burton's translation than most people.

"Whatever its flaws, it's an important part of English literature." He looked at the book contemplatively, the light from the lamp making his hair gleam like black silk. "Besides, the source material likely comprised many historical revisions of Vatsyayana's original work." His voice was pragmatic. "Although, they didn't have the same lasting consequences—it's possible that no other version of a book has ever so drastically altered the nature of that work on a world scale."

"How so?" she asked, intrigued.

"Have you read it?"

Alyssa shook her head.

"Most people think Kama Sutra is an erotic manual." He turned his head towards Alyssa. She met his gaze. "It's not. That belief is the legacy of abridged copies of this translation," he touched the book lightly, "that include only the chapters about sexual union. The Sanskrit manuscript encompasses far more. It was written as a guide to love. It's about courtship..." his eyes moved over Alyssa's face, "... seduction, marriage, emotional connection and more. Erotic pleasure is an important part of love," he paused, and there was something in his voice, "but it's not the only part."

Desperately, Alyssa tore her eyes away from Sai, focusing on the book that lay before them. As she turned the pages, she saw what he meant. There were no erotic diagrams—at least none so far. But the words were more powerful than any image could ever be. In an attempt to garner distance—emotional if nothing else, Alyssa began to silently read a passage on the open page: It is said by some that there is no fixed time or order between the embrace, the kiss, and the pressing or scratching with the nails or fingers, but that all these things should be done generally before sexual union takes place…Vatsyayana, however, thinks that anything may take place at any time, for love does not care for time or order.

Her lips parted softly as she re-read that last phrase.

She'd been wrong.

This was not creating distance.

She was more aware of Sai than ever before.

He stood at her side, and slightly behind, his chest grazing her shoulder. Then he whispered in her ear, "I've been reading this chapter." He turned to a new section. There was a title at the top of the page: On Courtship, and the Manifestation of the Feelings by Outward Signs and Deeds.

His voice was husky as he read. "The man should do whatever the girl takes most delight in, and he should get for her whatever she may have a desire to possess. Thus, he should procure for her such playthings as may be hardly known to other girls." He paused, and, unbidden, a series of leather-bound volumes flashed through Alyssa's mind. Treasures she'd only seen or possessed or held in her hands since knowing him. Sai's voice was a whisper as he continued. "He should try in every way to make her look upon him as one who would do for her…everything…that she wanted to be done."

She turned wide eyes to him but couldn't say a word.

Sai met her gaze, book forgotten. He took off his glasses and set them aside.

"Tell me, Alyssa. Is it working?"

She shook her head mutely. In slow desperation.

"Liar," he breathed.

Now he was reading her. Because she was a liar. What

he was doing worked on her from the very beginning. She'd simply been unaware he was doing it, and now, was uncertain how to respond.

"Why do you keep running from me?" he asked, softly.

Because she was afraid of feeling this way alone.

He was so close, and the desk was at her front. He didn't trap her against it—there was still a path of retreat. But his gaze held her spellbound as his head lowered. Alyssa trembled, and his eyes gentled. He cupped her jaw tenderly, slowly raising her face to meet his. Then his lips whispered against Alyssa's.

She stopped breathing.

The caress felt like butterfly wings.

Her eyes slid closed.

For long, seductive moments he pressed his lips to hers, moving them softly, slowly. Eventually, he pulled back.

Alyssa opened her eyes to find him a breath away. He looked at her, searching her face. Alyssa couldn't hide her reaction. Not after knowing the seductive enchantment of his kiss. She was powerless against it.

Against him.

He still held her jaw in his fingertips. It was the only place he touched her.

"Tell me to stop and I will," he whispered.

She looked up at him, helplessly.

"If you don't," he warned softly, "I'm going to kiss you again. And I'm not going to stop until you tell me to."

Time seemed infinite while he waited for her to speak. A log shifted in the fireplace, sending up sparks. The rain drummed softly against the window. The room was cosy…intimate…a world tucked away inside the world.

Sai searched Alyssa's face for a long time, but she remained silent. The silence lengthened until it became clear…she wasn't going to tell him to stop. Realisation crossed his eyes, and a faint sound escaped his throat.

He swooped.

This time, when his lips covered hers, the difference was immediate.

Seduction became demand.

Sai's arm banded her waist, turning her into his body. Her head fell back under his mouth, lips parting as she crossed the line she'd meant to never cross. His hand moved from her jaw to her caramel hair, still damp at the roots. He cradled her head as he kissed her, deeply, intensely.

Alyssa moaned, as though a long wait finally ended.

Her hands found his waist, resting lightly against the black jersey of his sweater. Sai explored her mouth, the plush wet silk behind her lower lip, the slick, sensitive interior, until she was desperate for more. Then she fisted the black jersey and raised herself on tippy toes, pressing her breasts against his chest and tipping her head back further, relying on the cradle of his hand.

Sai accepted the invitation, and the kiss turned dark…consuming.

The scent of Old Spice overwhelmed Alyssa's senses. She whimpered, deep in her throat, and pressed harder against Sai, suddenly, supremely aware of the lush fabric of the robe brushing against her bare skin, her tight nipples.

Sai stepped her back against the walnut desk until she could feel its edge. He lifted her with one arm and set her on the desk, in the pool of lamplight. His hips nudged her knees, and they opened for him as he laid her back, eclipsing her with his body. The robe parted at her thighs and her hair cascaded across the walnut surface like gossamer.

Sai kept kissing her, as though the world were ending.

In the last rational part of her brain, Alyssa reached out and pushed the cradle holding the leather-bound volume across the wide desk, until not even her fingertips could reach it.

Then Sai's arm shadowed hers and pushed it further aside, to safety.

That was all the consideration they could give it.

His lips finally broke from hers and travelled down her jaw, her neck, leaving a hot, damp trail in their wake.

Alyssa buried her hands in the silky black waves of his hair, tilting to give him better access. His mouth followed the edge of the robe down into shadows, pushing it aside as his lips traced the inner curve of her breast. Her hands in his hair tightened as desire gripped her, and her chest rose and fell underneath him.

Sai pushed the robe off one shoulder. His lips traced the hollow below her collarbone, and his hand cupped her shoulder, smoothing over the soft skin as though he couldn't stop touching her.

"You're so beautiful, Lyssa," he whispered, between kisses that stroked her skin like feathers. "Your eyes, sometimes amber, sometimes gold. Your hands, the way you touch a book, as though it's priceless."

Wonder flooded her.

"All this time…I wanted you to look at me." His words wrapped around her. "Touch me."

She slid one hand from his hair to his face, cradling his cheek, whispering her fingers across his skin. He turned into her hand, kissing her palm, her fingertips, until she was stroking her thumb across his full lower lip.

"All this time…I wanted to touch," she whispered, confiding the truth she'd hidden for so long.

His body tightened.

He raised himself a few inches and stared down at her face intently. Alyssa's breaths were heavy, then caught in her throat when she felt his hand at the knot in the robe's tie.

He pulled one end, slowly…never taking his eyes from hers.

It came free with a soft snap.

Alyssa trembled.

He slid his hand under the remaining half-knot, pulling it undone.

Then Sai straightened until he was upright. Alyssa's hands fell to her sides. She watched as he slowly stripped his black sweater over his head.

It was like unwrapping perfection.

Her eyes trailed across his wide shoulders, down his long torso to his narrow waist. He was lean but powerful, his skin burnished in the lamplight. She wanted to reach out and touch those toned muscles, all stamina and endurance.

He didn't give her the chance.

Sai reached down and parted the robe, spreading it wide until the plush material fell open against the glossy walnut, leaving her exposed to his gaze. For an infinite moment, his eyes moved over her, the banker's lamp casting her in a pool of light, like she was on display.

Alyssa bit her lip, eyes wide, and imagined what Sai was thinking as he stared down at her, at the way she lay before him, an invitation.

He reached out, placing his hand flat on the centre of her sternum, in the space between her breasts.

Her heart stuttered.

There was something about the way he touched her, as though he was gauging the rise and fall of her chest, her heartbeat. As though he'd wanted to touch her there forever. Then he closed the space between them and kissed her. His lips on hers were reverent, and intense emotion mixed with desire as Alyssa kissed him back.

When she felt his other hand on her ribcage, her belly clenched. He slowly moved up her ribs to her small, ripe breast. He cupped her, squeezing gently. Then his thumb brushed her sensitive nipple. Alyssa moaned into Sai's mouth, arching into his hand.

As though that was the signal for more, his thumb and finger tweaked her nipple softly, at first, then firmly, the hard pressure sending erotic sensations tingling through her body.

He kneaded and cupped and tweaked as he kissed her.

Until Alyssa was breathless, wordlessly begging.

Sai's lips left hers and trailed down her jaw, her neck, her shoulder, over the curve of her other breast. His mouth enveloped her puckered nipple, sucking tenderly. She buried her fingers in his hair, the sleeves of the robe falling down her arms. Her knee rose to grip his sides as she arched under him.

His lips trailed down her body, murmuring seduction against her skin. His mouth feathered over her flat belly, and her womb fluttered at the sensation. He grasped one of her legs, slipping it over his shoulder. The other, he spread wide, opening her.

His lips kept travelling south, and Alyssa's breath shuddered out as she realised his destination. When his mouth found her, she threw back her head, a broken moan escaping as she stared up at the ceiling, not seeing it.

His lips worked at her clit, laving, and sucking, one hand wrapped around the thigh at his shoulder, the other at her knee, holding her open as she writhed under him. He tormented the sensitive nub until her body was taut and her core ached, needing him inside where she was wet and empty.

"Sai," she moaned helplessly. "Sai."

He straightened, and Alyssa whimpered, but she remained open, even without his hold. His eyes dropped to her core as his hands went to his jeans. She watched through heavy eyes as he discarded them.

Her lashes fluttered.

His cock was thick and erect; as perfect as the rest of him. Her eyes barely found a moment to worship before he came to her, covering her body with his own.

His lips took hers, and his fingers found her heat. Two thick digits toyed at her entrance. Alyssa moaned as he penetrated her in a long, slick slide, her core wrapping tightly around the sweet invasion, reluctant to release him as he withdrew, desperate to welcome him as he returned.

For long minutes, that's what it was like, as Sai built her need with his lips and his fingers. But it wasn't enough. She needed him. Desperately.

"Please," she begged. The word was lost against his mouth.

But Sai heard, and, as she was learning, he gave her what she wanted. She heard a drawer open, and foil crinkle. Then the broad head of his cock replaced his fingers. Slowly, he pressed inside. Alyssa whimpered as she stretched around him. He was long and thick, and her body slowly yielded, just as her heart did.

His kiss deepened in time with his possession.

Until, after long moments, Sai was embedded inside her.

His hand buried in her hair, cradling her head for his kiss as he moved, each slow thrust possessing her completely, each withdrawal leaving her anxious for his next possession. There was nothing else in the world as Sai made love to her. Slowly, ardently, as the rain beat down on the window and the lamplight bathed them in gold.

She could feel the tension in him. The restraint. Until their need became urgent, and his pace increased. His hand burrowed under her back and wrapped around her shoulder, stopping her from sliding away across the polished walnut surface. Alyssa's nails dug into his muscular back. She locked her ankles low around his hips, working to meet his powerful thrusts.

Sai knew what she needed, and he took her thoroughly…completely…so there was nothing but him. The world passed by—it could have ended, and they would have never known.

Until Alyssa was on the pinnacle.

Sweat dampened her brow and glazed his shoulders as Sai buried his face in her neck, his hips working. His hand slid between their bodies, and his thumb stroked her clit.

That was all it took.

Alyssa broke; she cried out as intense pleasure overwhelmed her. Her muscles clamped rhythmically around him, pulsing in a release that was more intense than anything she'd ever known. She heard Sai's raw, satisfied groan as he thrust deep inside her and came, long and hard, his body shuddering over hers. And it was like being lost in a fantasy world, a place of magic and wonder, with just the two of them. A world written for them, where nothing and no one else mattered, where pleasure was infinite and unutterable, and love was the next page away.

For a long time, they stayed like that, sweat-dampened bodies pressed together on the wide walnut desk in the pool of lamplight.

Neither of them uttered a word.

Eventually, Sai straightened, taking Alyssa with him. Her legs locked around his waist and her arms wrapped around his shoulders as he lifted her. She buried her face in the crook of his neck. The robe was a cape down her back.

Sai carried her to the leather chesterfield. He lay them down with Alyssa stretched out along his body, their legs tangled. She nestled against him, staring into the flickering fire, while Sai toyed with the soft strands of her hair.

Time was lost…until the antique mantel clock quietly chimed the hour. Alyssa's eyes strayed from the flames to the silver dial.

It was late.

As though he knew her thoughts, Sai finally spoke. "I want you to stay."

The way he said it…her eyes slid closed. Alyssa nodded against his chest, where her head lay over his heart.

"I don't mean just tonight, Lyssa." His voice was rough. His arm tightened around her waist.

Unseeingly, she raised her hand to his face, her finger-tips a whisper, her words a promise. "Neither do I."

Then Alyssa fell asleep with Sai holding her, as though, in a room full of treasures, she was the most precious wonder of all.

Not the Usual Way

CELESTE DARLING

Rhett was already waiting on the leather chaise when Alys let herself in the side door.

The smoke-tinged glow of the afternoon's sun gave his dark-gold hair a reddish tint. It cast his handsome features in a feline smile as he rose from the chaise and set his book aside.

The sight of him, as ever, sent her pulse into a thudding tattoo. Or maybe it was the way his gaze skimmed over the light summer dress she'd worn that day. Like he was thinking about sliding his hands beneath the soft, swishy skirts and touching her straight off.

It wouldn't be the first time.

Alys kept her composure as he rose and came to her, leaning in to press his cheek against hers.

The crisp, clean scent of him caught at her senses as his hands closed around hers, and he murmured, "Put on what's behind the screen, Lise. Then bring me the cuffs."

The tone was gentle; the grip was not. Anticipation prickled across her skin as he let her go. She took a wobbly step back. But she walked steadily to the ebony-framed silkscreen standing across the corner of the room, knowing Rhett was watching her move. Her slim waist in the encircling belt, the gentle curve of her hips and butt, the shape of her legs as the skirt flowed silkily around them.

Behind the delicate embroidered silkscreen, a sheer black robe hung from the mannequin. Alys brushed it with her fingertips and stifled a shiver. It had no belt that she could see, so it would veil her so long as she was still but conceal nothing when she moved.

She looked back through the translucent screen, found Rhett sitting back on the couch, his chin resting in his hands, watching her.

Her body clenched, a sharp ache unfurling from the cleft between her thighs. With a deep breath, she hung up her purse and shed the dress, her bra, her pantyhose, panties, and heels. Then she slid the robe over her shoulders and stepped out from behind the screen. The cuffs were on a table on the other side of the room. The open edges of her robe fluttered over her breasts and belly and thighs as she crossed to fetch them, before coming to kneel before Rhett.

Their arrangement had been in place since March after a mutual acquaintance put them in touch. Every Thursday night from six until midnight, she was 'Lise' and he was 'Rhett'. They didn't need to know any more.

Rhett's eyes flared blue fire as she handed him the restraints then offered her wrists for him to put them on.

Tooled black leather, lined with suede, and embedded with a pair of burnished brass rings, they fitted perfectly around her wrists as Rhett did them up. His strong hands held them firm against her skin as he buckled them on.

"Did you get the promotion you were hoping for?"

The mundane question startled her. She'd revealed a

little of her work stress over their last few sessions, but she didn't expect him to ask.

"Not yet. Next week."

He lifted an eyebrow, asking for more detail.

Alys hesitated. At the start, they'd agreed no personal information, but at some point her reasons for needing to submit came out. By the time it had all grown too much to hold in, Rhett had earned her trust. She held off telling him too much, but this was important. Also, pathetically, she had no-one else to tell it to.

"They're bringing the director in on Monday," she said. "He'll make the final decision."

But she wasn't here to think about work—about the endless struggle it was to be strong and calm and cool-headed and *better* than her male colleagues—she was here to forget. So, when the cuffs were fastened, she tested their tightness as though she didn't trust his handiwork, her eyes never leaving Rhett's. Pique flashed in blue depths.

"Very well," he murmured, as he slid an arm around her waist, drawing her in against the hard planes of his body. "It's going to be like that tonight, is it?"

Alys didn't answer him as he bent his head and tasted her mouth. Mostly because it was hard to think with his lips moving skilfully against hers. And because he'd palmed her breast through the silky fabric of the robe, his thumb rousing her nipple with firm strokes.

He made it difficult to think straight.

Although difficult wasn't impossible.

She pressed a hand to the fly of his jeans, cupping hard enough that the length of him swelled thickly into her hand through the denim. Rhett broke from her mouth with a groan. A moment later, fingers closed tightly on her wrist, and he pulled her away.

"Later, Lise," he murmured roughly, the corners of his

mouth curving in a knowing smile. "You'll get all of it later, I promise."

Stepping away, he palmed something off the high arm of the chaise and came back, holding up a strip of leather so soft it draped over his fingers.

"This one shouldn't slip as much as the last ones."

Alys turned to let him tie the blindfold on. She felt the difference across her skin and hair immediately. There'd be no slippage. No betraying light through the thin silk to orient her in the room. No drooping of the silk across her cheekbones as Rhett rode her mercilessly to orgasm after orgasm. And no stolen glimpses of his head thrown back as she swallowed him deep—a golden god of sex and desire worshipped as he should be…

Now, with her world dark, she wavered on her feet, her balance unsteady until Rhett pressed up against her back. Gentle hands brushed back her hair, slid down to briefly cup her breasts through the fabric of the robe, slid lower to delve between her thighs where she was already wet and aching.

"Maybe I should take you now," Rhett murmured in her ear, parting her so the cool air caressed her intimately, one finger slicking dampness across her clit, sending jolting spirals through her belly. "Spend myself in you at the start, so you know you won't get any dick for a while."

"Like you take long to recharge," she muttered, then jerked as he scraped an electric fingernail down her.

Lightheaded and sharply roused, she took a moment to realise she was being propelled across the room. Rhett's hand on the back of her neck and the carpet beneath her bare toes were her only sources of orientation.

Her shins hit smooth leather, and her hands went down to balance herself as the fingers curled around her nape. He guided her over to the high side of the chair and pressed her forehead down to the pillowed arm. The robe shifted, sliding up her spine as his knee coaxed her thighs apart.

Alys quivered, knowing she was a blatant invitation—to fuck, to spank, to toy with until she was begging for release. The only question was how Rhett would begin—and how long he would make her ache before satisfying her.

Without warning, Rhett slid two fingers deep into her. She gasped, then moaned as he stroked into her sweet spot, spirals of sensation burgeoning through her body.

"I think I'm going to fuck you," he said, his voice gravel-rough and thoughtful. "I'm going to take my pleasure in you and leave you aching for more. And," he flexed his fingers, "I'm going to do it bareback."

Her breath caught. A month ago, when the pathology results of their sexual health tests were exchanged, and he'd revealed he wasn't seeing anyone else, she'd given him permission to skip the condom for anything but anal penetration. Yet he'd continued using the condoms, and while she'd entertained several fantasies about him pounding naked into her, she'd also been relieved.

Going bare was a new frontier in their 'relationship'.

"Lise?"

"Not bareback," she told him, then whined as Rhett's fingers stilled inside her. "Rhett!"

"No? You gave me permission."

"I didn't...I'm not sure..." Alys shifted her hips restlessly, wanting the movement back. She shimmied on his fingers, trying to—oh, yes, *that*, there! "Rhett!"

His fingers scissored hard inside her, another spurt of pleasure along with the arrowing ache piercing her body. "You're sodden for me, Lise—eager and soft. And you'll be softer and wetter still when I spill myself in you."

"I don't want—"

"Yes, you do." The softness of his voice made her shiver as he pressed against her spine, as much as the hand expertly teasing her nipple. "You're going to glory with every naked inch of me inside you, my darling Lise. And when I'm done, you're going to *beg* for more."

She whimpered as he pulled his fingers out of her, empty and wanting. The blindfold heightened her senses— the slither of cotton over his skin, the rasp of his jeans zipper, the scent of her arousal. The weight of him shifted the padded leather under her knees and Alys clutched the chaise arm for balance. Her insides were tautly wired, her senses on high alert. Then hands guided her hips into place, and the hot tip of his erection stroked her entrance, teasing her with the promise of skin-to-skin intimacy.

"So tense." One hand cupped her mound, firm enough to encourage, light enough to ignore. "Do you trust me, Lise?"

The phrase was a check-in. Anything but her safe word meant *yes*.

Did she trust him?

"Lise?" Maybe it was the blindfold making her hear things differently. She thought Rhett sounded hesitant, but his next words left her no room for question. "Impale yourself on me, Lise. Show me how much you want me naked inside you."

Dizziness threatened—then she realised she wasn't breathing and exhaled on a gasp.

She trusted Rhett. She wanted to feel him come in her body, no protections, no barriers. And she wanted him to feel her naked on him—to make him ache for her the way she ached for him.

So, she eased herself onto his cock and gave herself over to her Dom.

Hours later in her own apartment, Alys stepped out of the hot shower and dried herself off.

Her body felt tender and used, but her mind was clear.

Rhett was good at that. Good at making her forget everything she needed to be, good at finding that point where she was entirely given over to his whims. Good at satisfying her body—and then bringing her down from the endorphin high.

And he was good enough she'd started wondering what he was like in the rest of his life. She knew better than to pry or ask. He'd been clear he was in this for the scene from the start. Still, after their Thursday night sessions, Alys lay in the dark and wondered.

Maybe did a little more than just wonder.

She climbed into the clean softness of her sheets, the fabric smooth against her bare skin, then reached over to the bedside drawers. The leather cuffs—bracelets, really—weren't like the ones Rhett fastened around her every session, but they did the trick. The tight clasp of the leather against her skin was both a reminder and a comfort in the solitary darkness of her bed.

Although, as she drifted off, Alys tried not to think about Rhett sleeping beside her, his body crowding her down into the mattress.

"So, are you seeing Ms Thursday Night again next week?"

Bret looked away from the cricket showing on the pub screen and frowned at his mate. "Don't even start, Dave."

David smirked. "Look, with my love life in shambles, I think it's only fair that you share yours."

"It's not a love life." If only.

"Sex life, love life," His friend shrugged. "Are you still seeing Ms Monday Afternoon? Mr Tuesday Night? I know that *I'm* your Friday regular..."

Bret's glare didn't seem to do much to dissuade his mate from the topic. "You can't be that hard up, Dave. You're always swiping right on Tinder."

"Casual hook-ups. Fine if all you want is tail, but...I've had more. I want more. Even what you do with your harem is more of a relationship than Tinder."

Bret hadn't had a harem for the last five months; Lise had been his only submissive during that time. At first, the people he'd met seeking domination hadn't felt like a good fit. Then it had been because he didn't feel like taking on new subs. It was only since Lise gave him permission to bareback he'd realised the only woman he *wanted* to dominate was her.

The truth was Bret wanted to know the woman beyond the submissive since the day they'd met.

Within five minutes of meeting 'Lise', Bret would have happily crawled into her bed, entirely independent of any sexual scene she needed. Her outfit had screamed Domme —from the sleekly fashionable business suit to the heels that put her nearly eye to eye with him. Her lipstick was pristine, her winged liner perfect, and her purse for the day had been in a shade of suede that exactly matched her mouth. When they'd started talking, he'd realised she was poised and capable, with the calm of a woman who didn't need anyone's approval.

On the surface, she seemed an unlikely candidate for a submissive.

Yet Lise wanted someone to make her let go without having to pay the price of personal interaction, and Bret had been willing to take on that requirement.

It was nobody's fault that he now *wanted* the interaction.

He liked the glimpses of the brisk, composed woman who arrived at his house and left after she'd submitted to him. He wanted to know more about her. To take the time to know her as a person and not just elicit a submission from her, the way others did with their relationships in the scene.

Then last night happened.

Tell me how I feel in you.

*Hot. So big and real and...*Lise's voice hitched as she urged herself against him the second time. *I feel like I'm yours,* she'd blurted. A high flush stained her cheeks and shoulders and breasts. *Only yours.*

Look at me. He'd waited until her lashes swept up, until her blurry gaze met his, saw him. *You* are *mine.* Only *mine.*

Yes, she'd said. *Yes.* And Bret had ridden her so hard, he'd left bruises on the curve of her buttocks.

In the pub lounge, Bret shifted uncomfortably as his body roused. This wasn't the time, place, or company to get hot thinking about Lise. To remember the wild abandon of her submission last night, let alone how he'd dreamed of waking up with her curled trustingly up against him.

She wouldn't be around for several weeks.

I won't be coming next week, or between Christmas and New Year, she'd said as he'd seen her out.

January, then?

She'd hesitated a moment, then nodded. *I'll text you.*

Bret wondered if she really would.

Last night's sub-drop was brutal. Lise spent twenty minutes curled up on Bret's lap after they'd finished, her face half-buried in his neck, shaking. He'd wrapped a cotton quilt around her, made sure she drank a glass of water and ate a caramel slice. Then he'd held her and stroked her with all the tenderness he dared, until her trembling eased. Then she was ready to put herself back together and walk out of his life for another week.

He'd checked up on her earlier today with a text: *You ok?*

Six hours later, he still didn't have an answer. That wasn't like Lise. He texted a follow up, deciding if she didn't respond this time, then he'd call the woman who'd introduced them. Lise had named Esther as the emergency contact, and Bret had agreed to that. Esther had even checked up on him several times, the careful go-between for their dynamic.

"Anyway, *are* you seeing Ms Thursday Night next week?" Dave barely hesitated. "Because I already paid for a plus one for the Christmas party. Which is next Thursday."

"You want me to go as your date to your work Christmas party?"

"And I want Jens to chew on his liver," David said lightly. "He never liked you."

"So, I'm not just your beard for the Christmas party, I'm the beard that's supposed to make your ex jealous?" But a party next Thursday night would keep him from thinking about Lise. "As it turns out, yes, next Thursday is free."

"Excellent," David purred, steepling his fingers together.

Bret quirked a wry smile at his mate, then paused as his phone buzzed with a text message from Lise. *All good. Thx for asking.*

He stared at it for a moment, contemplating messaging her back to keep the conversation going. *Did you hear about the review?* Or *Hope you have a good Christmas.* Or—

"So," David said, casual and oblivious, "about Thursday..."

Bret exhaled and put his phone away. "All right. Am I there to start rumours? Or stop them?"

Alys usually enjoyed the office Christmas party. The directors booked a restaurant; everyone went to a paid dinner. It was casual rather than formal, but public, so people didn't usually make complete arses of themselves.

Usually being the key word.

"So," Ben slurred, "of course you liked *Wonder Woman* with those ball-busters in it, but I bet you don't even know—"

Alys was not in the mood.

Although the work review went well, she was on edge.

She'd not only been promoted but received a pay increase *and* been acknowledged by the director as the key person responsible for the acquisition of a new big-ticket account. Which was a cause for celebration, yes, but a part of her also wanted to see Rhett, share her news, and let herself go in the hands of her Dom.

Except that she'd chosen to attend the Christmas Party and was now stuck dealing with the fly in the ointment.

Ben had been an asshole about her success all day. Part jealousy, part injured male pride that they'd recognised a woman above him, never mind that he'd done sweet fuck-all in the presentations for the account apart from turning up.

"Hey guys," David from Marketing sauntered up, beer in hand. "How's the serenity?"

"Well, if we had any to start with," Alys said dryly, "it would be completely gone now—"

The words stuttered in her throat as she looked beyond David to the newcomer he gestured into the circle.

"This is Bret. He's agreed to be my plus one for the night."

Across the circle, Rhett's steady and apologetic gaze held hers as she struggled to remember to breathe.

Look at me.

Her body went hot, and her core throbbed. Rhett's— *Bret's*—eyes surveyed her. Scarlet top, deep blue leather jacket, sleek black pants that tucked into heeled boots, and the tooled leather cuffs that were the reason she'd chosen this outfit.

Something to anchor her when she couldn't get her usual release.

You're mine. Only mine.

Alys looked away.

"Unfortunately, no," David was telling the others, "we're just friends. He refuses to give in to the attraction between us."

"It's actually your terrible sense of humour that I can't stand."

She was used to hearing that voice giving her instructions, telling her how well she'd done, talking low and dirty in her ear as he moved inside her. Hearing it warm with laughter at her Christmas party felt wrong in so many ways.

"Are you feeling okay, Alys?" Madison, her PA, was regarding her anxiously. "Maybe you should have had something to eat before we left the office."

"I'm fine."

"She didn't eat today?"

Madison frowned at Bret's question. "I know she had coffee and a cake—"

"It's been a busy day." Alys took a deep breath and held up a hand to keep Madison from fussing any more. "I'm fine, Maddie. I'll be back. I just need a moment—"

At the line of basins in the restrooms, she undid the cuffs and thrust her wrists under the cool stream of water from the tap. She could do this. Rhett—*Bret*—wasn't her Dom tonight, just a guy out for an evening with a friend. And if she needed something to ground her after the week she'd had, well, that was why she'd worn the cuffs.

Still, when she judged herself okay to go out again, she hesitated over putting the wristlets back on. She missed the clasp of the leather against her skin, but it felt too much like a crutch, and she didn't need that, did she?

He was waiting for her in the elevator lobby outside the restroom corridor, leaning one shoulder against the wall near a large potted fern with his arms folded over his chest. The pose looked introspective, presenting him entirely differently—not a Dom, just a man. Then he looked up as she came out, and their gazes meshed. Her pulse raced, but she made herself walk towards him and hoped her steps were steadier than she felt.

"I didn't know that you'd be here," he said as she reached him. "I wouldn't have—" Colour touched his cheeks, and he looked away. "I wouldn't have accepted David's invitation if I'd known."

"It was probably going to happen sooner or later," she said lightly.

"It's never happened to me before." He looked her over, taking in the details of what she wore. His eyes narrowed. "You're not wearing the cuffs."

His voice fell into the tone he used when he was dominating her, sending spirals of anticipation through her skin. *Not here. Not here.*

"Stop,' she said, her skin prickling hot. "You don't have to play out a scene for me here."

"I'm not.' Then his fingers slipped around to encircle her wrist, a warm fetter that loosened her insides. "I just noticed it."

"Bret." His real name came so easily to her lips. "Please don't. I don't want—I can't—"

He tensed and let go of her immediately. "I'm sorry," he murmured. "About tonight. About last week."

"It's not—" She made herself look him in the eye. "This isn't about last week. It's about...It's about keeping things separated. I can't—I can't be known to—"

She might as well have slapped him. There was a moment of shock, and then his expression cooled although the high flush on his cheeks remained.

"I apologise." His voice was brutally restrained. "I won't bother you again tonight."

As she watched him stride away towards the dining area of the restaurant, the warmth in her insides transmuted to a tight ache. Everything around her suddenly felt razor-sharp, hot and cold all at once. She nearly called him back, but that would draw attention and she just couldn't. They'd already gotten a few curious looks from people passing through the elevator lobby.

Going back into the restrooms, Alys put the leather wristlets back on, strapping them a little tighter. The pressure on her wrists anchored her, at least until she joined the others at their table. One glance across the room showed Bret sitting with David and others at the second table. His gaze dropped to her wrists, and his expression froze. Then someone said something to him, and he looked away and laughed with the rest.

Alys found a seat with Madison and the other women and tried not to hear Bret's laugh at the other table. Or remember the look in his eyes that seemed oddly like betrayal.

I need to apologise. Can I see you now?

Alys told herself it wasn't likely Bret was up. He'd left the party almost as soon as they'd served dinner, and it was nearly midnight now. Slipping the phone back into her purse, she stared blankly at the screen at the end of the train carriage as it announced the next station stop.

Her phone buzzed.

Thursday nights are yours, 5pm until midnight.

She nearly ran to her car from the station, then drove like a madwoman to his house. The porch light came on, and so did the light over the path leading to the side door in the library.

It was one minute to midnight when she typed in her code and let herself in the door.

Bret was waiting for her, sitting on the chaise with a book in his hands, his face carefully expressionless.

For a moment, she hovered, uncertain. Despite the familiarity of where she stood, everything felt different.

"What did you want from me tonight?"

He blinked, surprised by her opening. His mouth quirked. "That's usually my question."

"That's why I asked." Alys took a step into the room. "I'm sorry I brushed you off. You took me by surprise."

"And you didn't want your colleagues to know. I understand." Bret closed the book and put it neatly down on the end of the lounge. "Tonight, I wanted..." He hesitated, then shrugged. "I wanted to have a conversation with our clothes on. I wanted to talk like we were just people. Not dominant and submissive playing a game in public."

His eyes met hers, and it surprised her to see a flush rising beneath his collar.

"I've wanted it for a while."

"Conversations with our clothes on?"

"I like the woman who trusts me with her body," he said, gentle but forthright. "I've been thinking I'd like her to trust me with other parts of her life. But how do I suggest that when I don't even know her name?"

"You know my name now. And where I work." Alys held herself still, but Bret's gaze sharpened, accustomed to watching for her cues.

"I promise not to use it against you. I wouldn't."

"I know. That's not it." She hesitated, then crossed the room to sit beside him on the couch. "I've been wearing the cuffs to bed after our sessions. *Just* the cuffs. I needed the grounding."

Bret took her hand in his, lacing their fingers together as he turned her hand so he could see the leather. "Do you need it tonight?"

"Yes." His hand tightened on hers, and he stood, pulling her up. Alys dragged on his hand, making him sit again. "Wait. I don't want to—I mean, I do. But not the usual way."

He stared at her for a moment before a slow smile grew on his lips. "Then I guess you're in charge now."

Apparently 'not the usual way' didn't mean she would stay clothed.

Yet when Bret voiced his apprehension as she pulled her top over her head, Alys put her hand over his mouth and waited. He looked into the wide and wary blue gaze and then kissed her fingertips in acceptance.

The submissive who trusted him to control her pleasure was still here, but she wouldn't give way to him tonight.

She stripped down to her skin, standing in nothing but the bronzed leather cuffs. The look in her eyes challenged Bret to do something—touch her, kiss her, fondle her, take her over his knee—but he wanted to know the woman beyond the submissive more. So, he returned her look and waited.

After a moment, Alys stepped in and undressed him.

Button by button, she undid his shirt, never looking away from his face. Her knuckles grazed his pecs as she slid the shirt off his shoulders, her fingertips brushed his hips as she divested him of his trousers. Bret felt stripped naked, bared to the soul and not merely the skin.

When she rose onto her bare toes and smeared a kiss into his mouth, her breasts stroked him like points of lightning across his skin. Bret caught her head between his hands and lingered in the kiss, tasting her—*feeling* her—as thoroughly and lingeringly as he'd wanted to but never dared.

When she backed him up against the chaise, he went willingly, the leather beneath him cool against his thighs and buttocks. She mounted him, pressing his hands to her hips as she rubbed her silky hot cleft against his dick and licked her way into his mouth with a murmured, "Take me."

Bret needed no more encouragement than that.

It was an intimacy they'd shared plenty of times before, but which felt different tonight. More than the slick, bare heat of her surrounding him, more than the rub of the cuffs pressing against his shoulder-blades as she clutched at his back. More than the intensity of her gaze and the need in her voice as she rode him to a slow and thorough ruin.

Bret didn't have the words—or the breath—to describe

what 'not the usual way' meant as she stretched out on him afterwards. Not then.

Not until the next morning, when he woke with Alys sprawled against him in bed, naked but for the cuffs around her wrists.

Not just like she was his, but like he was hers, too.

A Contract to Love

I M JASPER

Chapter 1

Thump, thump, thump.

Hear that?

That's the sound of my head banging on the table because I've broken the one cardinal rule of prostitution. I've bloody well gone and fallen in love with my client.

It's my own fault, really. He's recently gone vegan and requested I go vegan the days I see him. Of course, I agreed. When you're being paid $5k for the night, you have to be open to special requests. And let's be real for a moment, it's hardly the wildest kink in the jungle. I told him I'd do it, but I expected him to pay for two days if he was expecting me to vegan-ise myself for our appointments.

He smirked and shook on it, handed me more cash than I could've made in a month at my old job, and said he intended to get his money's worth. Now it's been four days at his beck and call and I'm officially in hell.

Assuming hell is the place you go for outstanding sex.

There's a reason he's my favourite client; nine-and-a-half-inch cock with enough girth you might cream yourself just looking at him. That's if his silver fox, movie star good looks hadn't already gotten you wetter than wet. Oh, and he's a millionaire who could have any woman in the world. But he's paying me to fuck him.

And that's the biggest turn-on of all.

Whoa, now don't go getting all '*Aww it's just like Pretty Woman*' on me just because I said he's a rich silver fox and I'm a prostitute. It's nothing like that. Any misconceptions you have about poor, damaged souls, victims of addiction and trafficking? That's not me. I'm privileged. I'm rich. I was a moderately successful law graduate, but the idea of spending the rest of my life thinking in six-minute increments bored me to tears.

From bored to whore might seem like a leap to you, but a water cooler discussion had me nodding along, mentally spending my bigger cash flow. One of the more lecherous bosses at work suggested sex might get us a better bonus. It was met with complete condemnation from everyone else. When someone said, "We're lawyers, not prostitutes!" something clicked and the rest, as they say, is history.

The intercom buzzes twice, his code for hurry up and get naked. I climb onto the imposing mahogany table in the dining room of the luxurious penthouse he calls home. Dropping my silk robe sexily off my shoulders, I spread my legs, using the hideously uncomfortable chairs as a footstool for my sky-high leather stilettos.

Wait...shit...leather!

I scramble to wrench the shoes off my feet and throw them into my, oh crap, also leather handbag. The electronic lock whirrs. The only thing I can do is become a master of the artful drape and hope my robe will hide the evidence long enough to greet him, completely naked and hope he's alone. Or not. Sometimes it's more fun when he brings a friend.

Plus, I charge extra, like when a hotel charges you for the rollaway bed, it isn't full price but you're paying more than you rightfully should.

I lean against the wall, in full view of the front door, stark naked and juices already dripping at the thought of what awaits me.

"Kitty." He smiles, wolfishly.

Oh, that's a very good sign.

"I wasn't expecting you to be home, you'd better put on a robe, we have a guest."

He doesn't want me to put on a robe. If he had, he wouldn't have buzzed twice.

"Oh, don't bother on my account, Leo." A man follows him in, older and less distinguished. He has an air of resentment and the red bulbous nose of someone who has had a few too many wines with lunch on a few too many occasions. "I presume, given my past dealings with your father, that you are paying this lovely young lady to seduce me into signing the papers?"

There's a flicker in Leo's eye, then he shrugs, neither confirming nor denying.

Did I mention he's enigmatic? He uses silence and ambiguity to lure his prey into revealing their intentions without them realising they're filling in all the blanks and building his arsenal of weapons to use against them later.

He's a ruthless businessman. I'd imagine most million-aires are. It's one of the things we have in common, or so he says. The night we first met, I was on another job and he picked me as a pro straight away. Said he could see that detached callousness, that do whatever it takes for financial gain attitude. He knew he could trust me to never fall in love or get the wrong idea about him or what our relationship was.

Obviously, he overestimated me.

"Kitty."

The way he purrs my name as he loops a finger through my necklace to tug me closer to him makes me weak at the knees.

"Silk isn't vegan." He points at my robe.

"Really?"

What the hell am I meant to wear to be sexy if silk and leather are off the table? Can you imagine phone sex without silk and leather when asked what you're wearing? Ooh, baby, I'm naked except for the 90% cotton polyester blend panties you like so much. I got them on special, three pairs for a tenner at Tesco. And the shoes are pleather, they don't breathe at all and it's disconcertingly sweaty in there.

I giggle. Urgh, see what he does to me? Giggling like a schoolgirl and completely side-tracked from the job at hand. Focus!

"You'd better not be laughing at me, Kitty." His eyes sparkle, not a hint of the cold-blooded businessman in them.

"Or what?"

"Or I'll have to punish you." The other man chimes in.

I'd forgotten he was there.

"Sounds like fun."

I'm not lying as such, but I'm not telling the truth either. This man, he's like a mosquito. Buzzing around, interrupting my moment with Leo. But squishing a mosquito is satisfying. Mosquitoes are the deadliest animals on earth. Whenever you squish one, you're practically saving a life. And that's why I'm here. I'll squish this mosquito until I save Leo from whatever threat he holds.

"Where do you want me, Leo?" The man sneers. "I'm ready to get royally screwed over in every sense of the word."

In Leo's office, vast floor to ceiling windows look down on the city skyline that's partially obscured by privacy blinds. Blinds Leo can control with a button under his sturdy antique desk. All whilst leaning back in his new mesh chair —not quite as imposing as the old leather one he got rid of last month. In fact, he's purged his entire office and home of all leather goods, except for the planner I bought him. That's still sitting right in front of him.

The boobs Leo bought me slap the man's face as he motorboats them like a teenage virgin with no idea what the hell he's doing. But I'm not focussed on him. My eyes are locked on Leo's. Knowing he's watching me, his hand rubbing up and down the glistening shaft of his cock, synchronised to me bouncing up and down on this other man's lap.

He licks his lips and I gasp, my muscles clenching, wishing they had Leo's massive cock to cling onto. A bead of sweat builds on his brow as his hand rotates around the head then pumps harder, faster. Now I'm the one trying to keep up. I tweak my nipple, and he groans. I arch my back, pointing my breasts in the air, my mouth partially open. If I wasn't fucking someone else, I'd be kneeling in front of him, begging him to shoot all over my face and tits. He knows what I'm thinking, it's written all over his face as I fondle my nipples until they are so hard, they ache.

"Let's sign the papers now." With unexpected strength,

the man I'd almost forgotten was there, lifts me up and sits me on the desk.

I turn around and get on all fours, not wanting to miss a second more of Leo jerking off. The man moans and spanks me.

What is it with middle-aged failing businessmen and spanking? I bet none of them are going vegan, just on the off chance they get the opportunity to break out a leather strap and spank someone with it.

"Hands off, mate," Leo growls and my legs turn to jelly.

They slide out from under me till my thighs and pussy rest on the desk. I'm gazing straight into Leo's eyes and everything but him fades into the background.

"I'm going to fuck you up the arse."

Fucking Mosquito Man ruining our moment yet again with a statement, not a question.

Leo holds his hand up, a physical gesture to shut Mosquito man up. My juices leak out, Leo's silent protection and strength make my heart sing and my pussy zing.

"Why shouldn't I fuck her up the arse whilst you screw me over?" Mosquito Man whines like an entitled brat.

"I have your permission. You don't have hers." Leo stands up, fists resting on the edge of the desk. He leans forward, remarkably authoritative for a man whose cock is swaying in the air-conditioned breeze.

"Can I..." he trails off, back to teenage virgin awkwardness.

I nod, and Leo releases a guttural groan. I swear his cock expands even more when he picks up the bottle of lube and dribbles it between my cheeks. The cool fluid leaks down to meet my fingers ready to massage it into my hole.

Pushed aside by the man, just as the pressure from my

fingers were taking me closer to the edge, I look up and am greeted by Leo's cock. My tongue thrusting out to catch the tip and lick the salty, creamy droplet of pre-cum off.

"I've never come in someone's arse before." The mosquito's voice is shaky, and Leo pulls back.

Seriously? Is he going to interrupt every moment I get with Leo today?

Sulking, I pout at Leo. His eyes sparkle like he's amused. *Patience, Kitty. Enjoy yourself.* I'm not sure if he actually mouthed it or if it's just wishful thinking as the sensation of a cock sliding in and out of my arse becomes harder to ignore. I need Leo. I need his cock inside me. The thought of being spit-roasted over this desk...

With his clean hand, Leo picks up some papers and balances them on my back. His slippery, lube covered hand encourages my mouth onto him—finally! The sweet relief of being able to lick, suck and kiss his cock.

The pressure of the pen digging into the paper scratches my back, adding to my high and overloaded nerves. There's something about the stretching of my arse, a taboo naughtiness in admitting I love everything about anal. Especially the tightness where even the smallest of cocks can still make an impact, fighting against my clenching sphincter. In contrast, my jaw aches as I accommodate Leo, my tongue circling the tip then bobbing down the shaft till he hits the back of my throat. I reach down and ram my fingers inside my soaked pussy, my thumb strumming my clit until every muscle clenches. I shudder and cry out, provoking an arse-slapping grunt of orgasm behind me and Leo who has both hands now cocooning my head as he thrusts and shoots inside my throat.

Fuck, I love my job.

Chapter 2

I stagger out of the office. The mood is all business in there now and I'm just a hooker, as easily disposed of as the used condom wrapped in a tissue in my hand. Tears sting my eyes and I blink them away, disposing of them as easily as I dispose of the condom into the garbage bin at the door that separates his work from his life.

What the hell is wrong with me?

I keep it together until I know I'm alone. Sliding down the bathroom door, I bury my head in my arms. My hands dragging through my sweaty, knotty, and tangled long hair.

Business Leo is not a post-coitus cuddler. I try not to wish he was. I'm a professional. I shouldn't need snuggles and warm caresses from a client. I most certainly shouldn't want them from him.

People say that once you develop feelings for a client, you've either got to give them up or give up the game. But I'm not ready to do either. Prostitution meets my needs— financially and sexually—but saying goodbye to Leo? A sob burns my throat.

Saying goodbye to Leo isn't an option. Not when he's the only man I've ever met who seems to see me as I am. Another sob shreds through me, because it isn't really my choice, is it? And how can I expect him to want the woman he just paid to fuck another man?

A door slams and I crawl into the shower. Tears trickle down my face, washed away by the hefty stream of water, no reduced flow showerheads around here. The cold tiles bite against my skin from below whilst the water burns from above. It feels oddly cathartic, a literal representation of my current purgatory.

Oh, snap out of it, Princess.

Even I'm sick of hearing myself whine. I stand up and

snoop through his bottles of toiletries. It's like someone bottled power, prestige, and a pine tree. It's probably advertised with a masculine man revving a fast car then driving along a mountainous road whilst the voice-over seductively whispers: *Douche gel for the Douche Canoe in your life.*

A knock at the door stymies my snigger.

"Kitty?"

He sounds hesitant. Who else is he expecting to be in here?

"Yes?" I step out of the shower and encase myself in a towel larger than my first apartment. There are probably small countries whose entire housing crisis could be solved with this towel. It's so disgustingly decadent, I want to be appalled. But secretly, I'm loving its warm embrace.

"I thought you'd left."

"Oh." Thought or hoped I'd left?

"Then I saw your non-vegan silk robe."

I grimace. I'd hoped he'd forgotten that. I open the door. He leans against the frame, my robe in his hand.

"Of course, then I found these…"

My leather stilettos dangle from his fingers. Bugger.

"Leather isn't vegan, Kitty."

"In my defence, I was out shopping for vegan approved clothes when you rang, and you said it was urgent. I didn't have time to change."

"Put them on."

I back up until I'm sitting on the vanity, my legs swinging in the air, the towel pooling on the counter.

"Make me."

He crosses the room in two strides. Heat prickles my skin and my pussy throbs. This is what I came here for. My fingers slide along my dripping pussy. He likes how easy I am. Likes that I'm ready and waiting whenever he's willing.

He'll whisper that it turns him on, then back off muttering that's probably why I'm good at my job.

I know that's what's about to happen because that's what's happened a dozen times before. I live for that moment. When it's just us, him and me, alone and in lust.

"Fuck you turn me on, Kitty." He nuzzles into my ear, then stiffens and steps back. Focused instead on strapping the leather stilettoes to my feet.

With one leg draped over his shoulder and the other wrapped around his waist, he traces along my thigh and around my vulva with his sheathed member. I can't feel anything except the burning desire to have him inside me. Fucking me hard and fast until the furniture starts to break.

"Make love to me."

The whispered words hit me like a sledgehammer.

"Just today, make love to me. Not because I'm paying you, but because you want to."

There's a quiver in his voice, and his eyes are locked on mine.

My leg slides off his shoulder and down his arm. I tell myself I'm doing it to appear less like I'm shamelessly anticipating sex and to look more like a demure lover. But my throat feels tight and I struggle to breathe. I'm pretty sure I'm nodding.

When his nose bumps against mine, and he kisses me, my heart skips a beat. His soft lips surrounded by a hint of stubble are everything I've ever imagined. Our tongues touch and we both pull back, overcome by shyness. There isn't an inch of his body my tongue hasn't explored, except his lips and mouth—until now—and this is when I get stage fright?

His hands cup my face and I'm mesmerised as his eyelashes tickle my cheek. I close my eyes, inhaling his scent and relish his breath against my skin between tender kisses. His lips meet mine and I wrap my arms around him, my fingers massaging his head through his soft, silky hair. I'm holding him to me, not wanting to ever let him go. I can feel his hardness straining against me, and I shift. He moans into my mouth as he stretches and slowly fills me.

His hands trace down my back, then grip my hips, the tenderness broken by desire as he wrenches me forward off the vanity and thrusts hard until his balls slap against me. The thwacking sound makes me laugh, even as my body convulses and my legs clench around his waist. The spike of my stiletto meets soft resistance. But the throbbing inside my pussy is all I can feel besides the cool mintyness of his tongue and the warmth of his lips against my own.

My foot bumps against something and I open my eyes, discombobulated to see the lounge room disappear behind us. I spin around as much as I can without letting go of Leo, whose shoulders shake with silent laughter.

"I said I wanted to make love, Kitty."

His eyes sparkle and oh, that smile. I bite my lip because his smile makes me happy. Happier than I'm allowed to be.

"Uh-uh. Don't do that." His arm shifts, embracing me tighter, pinning me to him. His hand brushes a hair from my face. "Don't shut down."

I freeze. It's like he can read my mind.

"Oh, come on. That wasn't meant to make it worse!"

He's laughing at me, I know this because even though I'm not looking at him, his cock is twitching in time with his shoulders, and it kind of tickles.

Now it's my shoulders shaking, and pelvic muscles clenching. I duck my head against his chest, so he can't see my face. His lips brush my hairline, and he lowers me backwards. It's a movement I hate. It feels like I'm falling.

Normally I'd sweat, my heart would race, and I'd be fighting, desperately trying to gain a sense of control.

But none of that happens.

The softness of the bed surprises me. I've fucked Leo in what I thought was his bed before. It's a huge king-size bed in a room that screams minimalist millionaire. Not a hint of personality, all cold, hard lines including the bed. But this is soft. Really soft. Fluffy even. Unlike his cock which he just withdrew, leaving me hollow.

"You're not helping."

"What?"

I'm too busy looking round to listen. There're dozens of photos lining the walls, mostly sepia-tinted old photos depicting laughing children and dogs, but there are a few newer ones too. Including one of me. A selfie of us pulling faces with ice cream smudged on my face. It was taken last summer. He'd offered to walk me home after screwing me. I'd been dubious, I never took clients home. That was my sacred space that no one was allowed to enter. But I'd relented. We'd bought ice creams for the walk and I'd stumbled just as I was about to lick the ice cream and ended up wearing it. He'd laughed that hard he ended up crying. It was the first time I'd seen him not scowling or serious. Until that moment, he'd even done sex earnestly. I took him home that night, into the sanctuary, and we'd shagged. It was playful, fun, and completely life changing. That was the night I'd first fallen in love with Leo and my heart hurt at the thought of how rarely he showed that side of him.

He tugs at my leather stiletto, yanking me back to now.

"What are you doing?"

"Getting rid of these vicious, non-vegan leather, instruments of torture."

There's a stiletto heel sized welt on his thigh, a droplet

of blood oozes from it. Good thing we aren't on the crisp white sheets of his other bed.

"Sorry."

"For lying about trying veganism and wearing leather." He grins. "Or for inflicting grievous bodily harm."

"Both."

He laughs.

"What?"

"Liar."

I want to argue but my leather shoe comes off my foot and, in one swift movement, Leo has thrown them off the bed and me back against the pillows. His tongue flicks against my nipple, and I arch my back. Holding his head, begging him to suck and bite harder. His fingers dance around my pussy and I clutch his wrist, desperate to have them, him, inside me.

Holding hands, our fingers intertwined, he moves so my finger and his slide inside me. The heat of my wetness welcomes and envelops us. It feels incredibly intimate to be joined like this inside me. The muscles tighten and release around our fingers, the sensations from my hand and my bits are intense. My hips are rocking, and I don't know or care how many of our fingers are locked inside me because I'm grinding against our hands and I'm struggling to breathe. I arch my whole back off the bed and I'm going to come. Waves of heat radiate through my body. I shudder and jerk, unable to control my moans or stop my nails from digging into the back of his head as I smother him with my boobs.

The heat and pulsating throbs of my pussy have barely subsided when I feel his cock pressing into me. I roll so I'm now straddling him. Sliding up and down his shaft until he's completely inside me and I'm rocking my hips. Contracting and releasing, tight then tighter on his cock and the pulsating is like a time bomb waiting to explode, ticking down the seconds. My bucking on his boner bringing me closer to the edge until I can't take anymore. My entire body throbs and I can't hear from the blood pounding in my ears. A single droplet of sweat trickles down my spine, sending my skin a thousand alerts that spark goose bumps and shivers of ticklish satisfaction.

My breath is ragged as I'm flipped over, and he starts thrusting. His hands hold mine above my head and we're kissing. I'm lightheaded and my body feels like jelly. I don't think it's possible for me to orgasm again but then his cock thrusts just as our tongues meet and my muscles contract forcing my back to arch. I free my hands and drag my nails down his back, everything clenching just as his face contorts and grimaces. He collapses on top of me, sweaty and puffing. Both of us struggling to breathe.

Alone in the bed, I examine the room. It has an almost childish quality to it. It reminds me of my room when I was sixteen. A carefree optimism of what might be, happy memories interspersed with a clutter of things I wouldn't have expected, like toy cars. A large photo of a polo player whacking a ball at full gallop across a dusty field dominates the closest wall. On closer inspection, the rider is Leo.

"Hello, you."

His voice is quiet, and he's blushing. He's wearing boxer shorts and has disposed of the condom I was too exhausted to deal with.

A series of light kisses dot my shoulder and we snuggle into each other, like two pieces of a puzzle that join together perfectly. His fingers caress along my arm and my chest seems to expand with each beat of my heart, drumming him into my soul.

"I like this you." The words slip out before I've thought them.

He sighs. The caresses and kisses stop, and I hate how disappointed I am that this is all over. That he'll get up, offer me a bonus to remind me this is a financial arrangement only. Then he'll walk out, and I'll be expected to leave. Just like every other time.

But I can't do that anymore. I'm too far gone down this rabbit hole of love and affection.

"I do too."

The words are whispered, and I barely hear them.

"You do too, what?"

"Like this me." His nose traces along my shoulder before he abruptly gets up. "Why are you here? Is it just the money?"

The words come out rapidly, like machine-gun fire, and I wonder how to answer. Honestly and destroy what we have? Or lie and destroy what I'm wishing might be?

"I don't care about your money, Leo."

"Would you stay even if I couldn't pay you?" He's pacing now.

I nod, hesitantly. He sounds so earnest. I can't help but wonder if this is a trap.

"You know of my father?"

Again, I nod. Every muscle tense and on edge.

"He'd sell his soul for money if he could. He's a cruel and unforgiving arsehole and the thought I'm like him disgusts me." There's venom in his words. "I don't have any friends or relationships because I can't trust anyone's motivation for wanting me."

The bitterness and sadness I can hear makes me want

to hug him, but I stay still and silent. Maintaining professional boundaries.

"Except you. I trust you implicitly and I don't understand why." He kicks my stiletto, pointedly.

"If I was going to breach your trust, I probably would've done it by now." I stare out the window to avoid looking at his raised eyebrow.

The mattress sinks, and there's a kiss on my shoulder.

"I'm quitting."

"What?" I turn around so I can see his eyes.

"That man today? I destroyed his company. I killed off his livelihood. I ruined him. Because my father told me to. Because he could. Because I could."

He says it so coldly that I pull away.

"I don't ever want to do that again and the only way I can see to get out is to quit. But my father will destroy me, the way I destroyed that man today. He won't hold back."

I stroke his face, wishing I could make this better, but I'm just a prostitute. A business transaction he's building up to letting go. Because that's all I will ever be to the only man I've ever loved. He's moving on to a life that won't include me. I roll over, so he can't see my tears or notice my haunted breaths.

"Kitty, I'm in love with you."

"What?"

I yelp out the word. My eyes are so wide they feel like they might fall out of my head. My heart is pounding and the blood rushing through my brain is making my ears throb. I roll back towards him. He's pale and I feel a little sick at what he might say next in case I was imaging it.

"I love you. I love the way you make me feel. I love how you see who I am better than anyone. And I love that you make me want to be a better man. I want to be with you, like this, not just like..." He waves his hand towards the door. "I don't love your leather stilettos though."

"I thought you were ending our arrangement."

"I kind of hope that I am. If you'll have me as more than a client."

Now he's pulling away, blinking rapidly as though that'll hide the redness in his eyes. I lean in and kiss him, slowly, sensually.

"I love you too, Leo. Despite your aversion to my leather shoes."

Heavenly

ALLEGRA STONE

I didn't see my visitor at first, folded in between bulky bikie jackets and the waterfall of computer satchels. But I could smell him—a toxic mix of sandalwood and smoke. My eyes quietly scanned the store, tripping over and around the hellishly dull piles that made up my father's leather store Bonded. He had failed to see the name's irony.

An electric shimmer in the air, a dark hiccup in the space between us, rolled toward me as I caught the flash of tousled white. I slid my hand under the counter, grasping the end buckle of a size 36 embossed belt. As my fingers curled around its tip, I remembered the groans a similar firm hold had had on Tommy Hadly the previous evening. A small smile of satisfaction escaped at the memory of the lucky recipient's sticky introduction to adulthood. 'A birthday gift with compliments of your dad, Tommy,' I had whispered as the teen was going cross-eyed. Perhaps father and son were here for more. Together.

"I don't open until nine," I challenged into the darkness. My heart hammered against my shirt like Jessica Rabbit's. From anticipation or fear I couldn't say.

"I've come for some leather. You know what I need."

I gasped as the voice washed over me, around me, and eased its way into every crevice of my body. I knew its throaty tone but couldn't place it. Its lilt, mocking and personal, made my head swim. I fingered a pair of razor-sharp shears and eased around the counter.

The shop sat stagnant and humid, as though each leather garment still breathed. A lone fly buzzed along the windowsill; another anxious to leave. The distant snores of my father, hiccupping in last night's whisky, filtered down the hall from our premises. I flicked on the overhead light, again cursing its anaemic efforts to bring a little brightness into my life.

"I have no idea what you need," I ventured. "Perhaps you could show me."

The cluttered stock seemed to part like the Red Sea, but it wasn't Moses I saw uncurl. A glow from the rising sun misted through the grimy window, bathing my visitor from behind in a halo of Sicilian orange. He slowly stepped forward, giant tufted wings struggling to fully unfurl in the cramped store. The tips pushed against coats suspended from the ceiling, grotesque bats next to the beauty of his wings. Were they appendages? I shivered at the possibilities.

It seemed like minutes before he was fully raised, and he was beautiful.

"Are you from heaven or hell?" I drawled, settling on heaven with the wish for a bit of hell thrown in. I eased the scissors back under the counter, my palms slick. I reached back deep into my memory. A flash of feather, a muffled gasp of pleasure, cutting and punching tools strewn over the floor—I couldn't quite reach the moment.

In one strong stride he was against me. His skin was as

smooth as white alabaster, the shadows from his muscles smudged across his entire body. He seemed chiselled from ice, but menacing heat was what he projected. Bleached hair was cropped short against his skull, a single gold stud pierced one earlobe. My fingers tingled, eager to reach out, to run over every centimetre. His black eyes impaled me as they witnessed my every explicit thought. He oozed power and darkness.

"Why are you here again?" I teased.

He held my gaze, eased back and, with a sleight of hand any magician would covert, he unwrapped the tattered leather piece from around his groin. He held it out to me and said, "Take a look."

Which is exactly what I was doing, albeit a little lower. His V-cut pointed directly at his immense, and perfect, penis. Somewhere in the back of my muddled mind, a sense of the ridiculous surfaced. I wanted to adorn it, to drape a red feather boa around the shaft, to tickle its tip. I imagined his wings shuddering in unison, perhaps even turning a darker shade of evil as his blood pulsed. He shuffled his bare feet apart slightly, delighted in my inspection. Perhaps he could sense my pulsating vagina or caught the slight scent of my wetness. Another step and he was against me, his hardness pressing like a metal rod. Desire surged painfully through my body as I tossed my head, as if it was only natural an angel appeared in our dingy little leather shop.

Effortlessly, he lifted me onto the counter, edging his body between my spread legs. It was like being pulled into a rip. You knew how it could end, but it was best just to be taken along.

He eased his erect member under the deep counter edge, closing his eyes at the pleasure of his own touch. I pictured it lying under there, waiting, pointing back towards the cash drawer. Kerching!

His calloused hands smoothed his leather across my lap, covering my entrance. Menacing enjoyment sparked in his eyes like lightning in a night sky. He had obviously seen my disappointment and frustration.

He flicked my black hair behind my shoulders, leaving his hand along the nape of my tingling neck. "Every year I come here to your little shop, and every time I would pay for a new warrior lap," he murmured. Somehow, I knew we weren't talking Australian dollars. He dropped his hand and presented me with the leather's branding mark. It could have been MacDonald's 'M' for all I cared; uninvited, fingers on his other hand were pushing aside my underwear, probing between my slick folds.

The townsfolk often commented I wasn't the smartest tool in the shed, but even I knew there was an expectation here. It was up to me whether I accepted the challenge. I brushed my hands up and over his chest, leaving behind a soft trail of light. He was cool to my touch, like a fresh gin and tonic on a summer day; mint replaced by his heady sandalwood scent. My eyes casually followed my fingers as they tiptoed out to where his wings peaked over muscled shoulders. A moment's hesitation, then the tips found spikey tufts, sinewy muscle, and soft folds of feathers.

"So, who served you before?" I asked, as my g-spot swelled, and my wetness threatened to spill across the counter.

"She's no longer here," he replied gruffly. "But you are."

I looped my hands behind his neck, my fingers toying with the bristled feathers that frilled there. His body took my weight as I eased my buttocks off the counter. A breath later, my pants were puddled on the floor amongst yesterday's offcuts. He lay his large hands over my full breasts, my pink nipples hardening unbearably. Shirt buttons magically popped off across the counter and onto the floor like the meatballs in that annoying song. My bra's front fastener sprung open.

He slid me forward, rough hands tilting my pelvis upward, forcing me back on my elbows. Metal filings dug into my buttocks, but now was not the time to complain. Quickly he looped thin thongs of tan leather around my ankles, fastening them to my father's cast iron stands. My legs were spread wide as the angel slowly lowered his golden head. First, he lapped at my wet labia, then took little bites of my exposed sex, before inserting his thumbs and spreading me wide. His hair was like fairy floss as I clutched it between sweaty fingers. A deep groan rumbled from my throat as I dropped my head back. His not-so-angelic tongue found my clit and when I bucked against the restraints, he continued to flick his tongue, snake-like in and out. I felt the pool of my release.

He uncurled, theatrically wiping away my glistening fluids from his mouth, continuing to pierce me with his stare. It all unfolded so quickly, as though he would move on with his otherworldly chores soon, maybe stop somewhere for a coffee and pastry. All my energy seeped out with my moans, leaving me quivering and prone; I was on earth, on the counter, in our shop, in a little country town. I shut my eyes, not sure if I was dreaming and if I wanted, in fact, to wake up. Where had he come from?

The ties slid apart, and my legs flopped down, waking up my body. It still writhed, wanting more.

"You want more?" he smiled, reading my mind. "Mmm, so do I." He gently pulled me upright, stood onto something and loomed over me. I glanced down, recognising my father's treasured upholstered footstool. Oh well. A flick of his hips and his hard penis sprung erect, tiny droplets glistening a warning. My hands reached out, unable to resist cradling his arancini-sized balls, stroking his silky-smooth member. I could feel the blood pulsating beneath the blue-rippled skin.

There was a rustle in the air as giant wings curled around, cocooning me in my task. My hands gripped the angel's buttocks—they felt muscled and warm, and I couldn't resist running my finger along their sweaty crease. I felt them clench but was focused on the ramrod shaft in front of me. In the soft, filtered light it was sublime, erect and waiting. I yearned to know what it would taste like— lemons, vodka, chilli, the salty sea or powdery clouds? My tongue teased the tip, circling around and around. I felt my head being eased down the shaft and gave in to rolling it in my mouth, sucking and nipping. I held his weighty balls, squeezing them lightly as I circled his penis with my fingers and eased away. My tongue ran the mile along the underside of his shaft; I was panting and needed to take a deep breath. The pair of wings quickly flapped back. A cracking sound echoed against my ears, through my mind. I glanced up into his bemused face—it seemed my technique wasn't what he wanted.

I couldn't say what flitted across his eyes at that moment. If the blackest of night skies could lighten a shade, then that was what transpired. A softness overtook him, and he stepped down from the stool.

"No wait," I stammered reaching for his cock once more.

It didn't diminish but lay erect against his rippled torso. The wings concertinaed around his back. His eyes flicked quickly to his abandoned leather cloth.

His earlier words echoed around my fuzzy brain. He's been here before? I glanced down at the faded leather. An embossed A mocked me through the wear and tear. Anastasia. My mother's brand. Well, at least it wasn't my father's.

"You fucked my mother?" I demanded.

As swiftly as he'd disrobed, he covered himself and stepped back. His eyes, hurt but dark once more, feasted on my body before turning away. I glanced at the windows, fearful the whole town was peering in, voyeurs to our actions, but they remained blank and dull. The morning had arrived, the earlier hush replaced with traffic and shouts. When I looked back, he'd silently vanished, a lonely feather swirling in the dust.

I can't say how I got through the remainder of the day. My body remained hot and slick despite a shower and change of clothes. I told my father I was unwell, but when I returned to the store, he had lined up the buttons from my blouse along the counter. Anger lit his every move until he moved on to the pub, leaving me amongst the musty leathers.

My sex throbbed as I propped behind the counter, using the rounded tools of our trade to climax, but I kept falling short of the delirious pleasure the angel had sucked out of me. I missed the unrelenting pressure of his thumb against my clit, his tongue stabbing and probing. His exquisite cock at home in my mouth.

Surprised at my descent into nostalgia, I considered his 'being'. Good Lord, was I thinking of his soul? My arms felt bare without encircling wings, my heart lifeless without a warm palm pressed against it. A certain glint I'd caught

in his eyes was not tied to sex or domination. It seemed…
caring. Tears smarted my eyes as I searched the drawer for
my mother's branding tool, but it was gone. Did she take it
when she disappeared one mysterious night six months ago
when she left behind her daughter? I curled in the corner,
naked amongst a pile of hides to endure another endless
night of darkness.

He didn't wait until dawn. His scent enveloped in the
middle of the night and I knew he'd returned. I tried to sit
up. He'd tied my wrists above my head with dog collars,
their diamante leads snaking away from my exposed body.
He squatted at my feet, his memorable cock and balls
hanging between muscled thighs. It wasn't his soul, or the
discarded leather, I was thinking about in that moment.

"Did you want me to come again?" he asked, his voice
gravelly and suggestive. A reddish glint against the black in
his eyes was new to me but promised another side, perhaps.
What that was, I wasn't sure.

I clenched my legs together in an inane attempt at
modesty. He flicked my feet apart and pursed his lips.

"I need to clear something up about your mother," he
began.

"Are you kidding?" I stammered. "What…"

The angel's face was stony as he stared me down.
Every insect, every dust mote stilled around us. In fact, I
was convinced the earth stopped rotating in that moment.
He was not to be trifled with.

"It's important to me that you listen. I cannot touch
you again or enter your body…" he whispered, running a
finger up the inside of my leg. It stopped just short of my
folds, then withdrew. "…or have you suck my juices," he
continued, "…until…"

"Until what?" I interrupted. Already I was wet, my
knees spread as I pulled against the leather ties.

In one liquid movement, he spread himself alongside me, his wings folded along his back. He reached behind me and gently rolled me toward him, his erect penis warm and throbbing against my trembling body. If my leg hadn't felt as weak as jelly, I would have thrown it over his thigh and pulled him closer. It always worked on other hesitant prospects. His 'do it and die' look made me lie still. My breasts thrust forward as the ties grew tighter with my roll, the nipples hard and tender.

He leaned closer. His mouth glided up my neck, tenderly brushing my lips with his own. If he'd thrust deeply into me, it wouldn't have stirred me as much as that kiss. It felt like the milky way, a new year sparkler and liquid hearts rolled into one. It was foreign, not part of my world nor how my life had unfolded. Day after day. Frowning, I struggled to be untied, but he hushed me. A surge of electricity zigzagged across our two bodies.

"She left me, not you."

Tears threatened, but I blinked them away. I refused to think about my mother when all I wanted was to work through what was happening. I wanted to be fucked. But more so, I wanted another kiss from this angel. Yet I needed to know.

"What do you mean?" I croaked.

"I visited her for many years," he replied, his hand stroking my hip. "I came upon your town, your shop, by accident one stormy night. I'd been thrown off my flight, had been battered and took refuge here. Your mother found me, healed me, although our injuries are quickly gone so we can be on our way. She made me the leather lap to wear as a reminder."

I lay still, my full breasts pressed against his hard chest. His eyes looked into mine, deep inside as though reaching in for a response, a recollection.

"There were other times you came during storms…I remember. My mother said I was dreaming, had turned me back to my room." But I remembered the wistful, sated look in her eye. I remembered the voices. He nodded.

"Then she changed. She demanded I stay," he scoffed. "Such an earthly vice."

"My father?" I whispered, fearing the worst.

"He saw us. I knew he was there, lurking in the doorway, jerking off as he witnessed me ravage his wife. I don't know if she welcomed me so he could watch, perhaps join in if I stayed, but I'd seen you. I needed to go, but I was weak."

At the hitch in his voice I leant closer, easing my knee to caress his cock. It lengthened at my approach, but his eyes said otherwise. He hadn't finished his story.

"Age stands still for angels, but you were growing, and she became more impatient, angrier. She wanted me here all the time. I feared she would set a trap for me. So, I didn't come. For many years I didn't come. But I would visit when she wasn't around, to watch over you. To protect you."

I jolted. "Untie me, you cocky son of a bitch," I demanded.

His expression changed, surprise and darkness taking over simultaneously.

"Untie me, I said. You couldn't fuck her any longer. You drove her away, leaving me with a drunk old father who couldn't get it up if he had a madam's ass sitting on his face. So, you think you can come back now? Now that the daughter's all grown up, and just take up where you left off?"

"That's not why I came back," he retorted.

His slender hands crept between us, poised against my nipples. They stood at alert, waiting. Ruthlessly, he pinched them. Sharp jabs of pain cobwebbed down my body as I held in my anguish. I strained forward, needing to take his lips in mine, to bite and smother his words in my anger. Easily, he turned his head away, then with lightning speed he pivoted across my body.

His knees lodged under my elbows, one hand held mine to the floor as the other eased his pulsating cock to the edge of my mouth. Gently he wiped my parted lips with it, and I felt his buttocks ripple against my chest. He towered above me like Goliath over David (if they'd been gay, that is), taking his weight on his strained thighs. His narrow aura pulsed a silvery grey, beautiful and erotic. It outlined his body, almost as a shield. My body writhed, both of us knowing it was from pleasure and expectation, not fear.

My tongue found the sensitive ridge around the base of his helmet. Around and around. He eased the hot rod into my mouth, inch by inch, then withdrew inch by inch. Greedily, I sucked the moisture from its tip as he reached a hand around between my parted legs. Warm, hardened fingers parted my humid lips as two digits hastily entered. His touch rocketed sparks through my whole body and I bucked with the pleasure of it.

His wings flicked open, heavenly in their expanse, shivering with every trawl of my teeth along his length. He grunted, glancing at my hands, and the leather fell away. I grabbed at his cock, his balls, regulating his entry into my spread mouth.

The angel smiled and eased away. Panic set in—was he leaving? Would he abandon me? I shuffled up, leaning my back against the grimy wall, and glanced at the doorway. I couldn't care what my father witnessed; but I knew he would drive the cutting shears into the back of my angel if he'd the chance. The miserly little store was empty except for the ripe smell of sandalwood and sex, and two bodies saturated in a sparking glow.

"Shall I turn you over?" he teased, standing over me.

His eye ran along the shelves of silky soft kid gloves and I thought I would come right then. But there was something in his eyes. Was this a test? Is he seeing what sets the daughter apart from the mother? My breasts ached. My pussy throbbed, but I needed more. I wanted this exotic stranger; I needed him not to stray.

I pictured myself, chin to floor, arse in the air as he took me —glove or no glove. A strap of leather between my teeth to quell the squeals of pain and delight. It wasn't what I wanted I realised, surprising myself.

"I want you to stay," I whispered.

The angel took a step backward, a frown of distrust on his beautiful face.

"No, no wait. Not like that. Not like my mother demanded. I want you to keep coming back." I couldn't keep the yearning from my voice. "Where do you go anyway?" I gave a short, mocking cough, suddenly aware that I lay exposed, my sex open for his eyes to continue to devour. I crossed my ankles. Demure. He smiled at my discomfort, making my anger rise again. "What? Do you just fly around until you see some poor female that needs filling with your ethereal juices?"

"Is there something wrong with that?" He cocked an eyebrow, running his hand down his engorged but dropped penis. "Isn't that a version of what you are doing right here, in the village?"

He did have a point.

"Okay, so if I can make your lap thing-o when you need it, will you come back?"

"Will you stop pawning yourself? You're beautiful, you know, but you have more. You're one of a kind."

I gasped, unsure of a response. My beauty had often been handed back to me like a trophy, a right of access. But 'one of a kind'. This was something else entirely. My hands clasped in frustration, my chest heaving.

"I'm just worried…"

"Ah, worry steals joy," he drawled. "Enough talk. Let's turn your worries into joy."

Despite his large frame, the angel was exceptionally flexible. In an instant he'd jerked my legs so once again I lay flat on my back; he registered I didn't want to be turned like a rotisserie chicken. The next moment he was lying along my length, muscled arms supporting his body above mine. Like push ups. He eased back, running his tongue along my stomach down to my pubic bone. A little shuffling and his tongue found its mark. Then he was above me again, staring into my moist eyes as he hovered. The restraint, the waiting, was unbearable. My efforts to pull him onto me were fruitless as he waited, his erection strong and long. I wondered if I could accommodate it. A groan of ecstasy echoed around the store, and I realised it came from my innermost parts.

I closed my eyes, feeling I'd my own little piece of heaven right here as my sex swelled and dripped. It felt the vibration and heat of the angel's penis before contact. I widened my legs in expectation. A quick thrust followed gentle circular motions around my edges before another deep thrust. It filled me, making me gasp. My eyes flew open as the slick cock withdrew and continued with its gentle massaging. The angel's eyes didn't leave my face, his hands holding the sides of my head, his elbows supporting his sliding body. We were both slick with sweat. Once again, he slammed into me and withdrew. My hips rose and fell to meet him as I gripped my raised knees in my hands. His wings stood erect, in a giant V.

Lightning penetrated the sky, sending shafts of white-hot rods around the street. A deluge flooded the streets—surely a reflection of what was happening in my vagina. His penis shimmered in the light. He continued to move slowly at first, edging in, thrusting, edging, then holding inside. He was inside me up to the hilt. The tip twitched inside me, rolling out spasm after spasm through my whole body. His cock felt chilli hot then ice cold as he increased his pace, ramming into me.

I'll be the first to admit to having a vast amount of sexual experience, of knowing just when, where and how to excite and withdraw. I can grip flexing muscles with my thighs and choke any penis with my pelvis, run a rough tongue anywhere and leave many panting. But this was out of this world. I could feel his insatiable lust all round me, within me, over me and under me; but at the same time, he was as slippery as an eel. An eel totally in control of the when, where, and how. He definitely had me at hello.

I screamed into the night in ecstasy as the angel shivered, then stilled. A low, long purr breathed across my face. He stayed inside me, erect, as his mouth searched mine, ravishing it with his tongue, his teeth, his kisses. If I looked down, surely there would be glitter pooled between my legs, sprinkled along my thighs like My Little Pony. I hadn't seen angel semen and nor would I, for as I looked down there was only my ejaculation slicking the hide.

The sweet smell of sex, of sweating leather, hope and exhaustion swirled around us. His mouth, now firm but gentle, found mine, nipping around the edges. I panted shallowly, trying to match his aura of calm. A tiny line of moisture across his chest, the only remaining sign of his efforts.

"I have to leave now," he whispered and rose effortlessly above me.

"No…" I tried to rise, my weak legs betraying me. I watched him wander past the counter, opening drawers swiftly. He dragged a new sheet of leather from its pole and lay it over his old one, cut it to fit. I smiled as he glanced down at me, seemingly proud of his handiwork.

"You should give Martha Stewart some tips," I joked.

"Who?" he asked, but his mind was on his task.

"Second drawer," I prompted. He shuffled through the tools, found what he wanted and branded me onto his leather. He ran his thumb over the initial. It was as if the hot initial had plunged against my own skin; I felt pain and heat soar through my heart.

"Z for Zoe. You've covered the whole alphabet, A to Z, with only two females."

My attempts at humour, to delay him, fell on empty ears. I knew that what I did in the next minute would set the plan for the rest of my life.

The leather bulged across his still hard penis. "When others come knocking, I won't spread my legs for any of them," I promised.

"I know," he nodded.

Cocky bugger, I thought. "But then again, what about the whole wing thing? I mean, you didn't put those feathers to much use, did you? Are you in training?"

His eyes darkened as, in a flash, he was around the counter and squatting in front of me. Quietly he plucked a feather from one wing, the others pulsating then readjusting to fill the space. He ran his fingers along the quill, forming a tip. One hand opened my labia as he trawled the feather through the sticky moisture. He lay it across my heaving stomach, then stood. A loud crack and shot of electricity throughout the room made me flinch; and in that blink he was gone.

"Next time," came a whisper. "I promise so much for next time."

Leather and Lacey

DAVINA STONE

LACEY

'Nat, can you come and help me? Pleeassse?'

I know I sound on the edge of hysteria. Hardly surprising considering my new jeans—bought especially for the Wallalinga High School Reunion—have shrunk.

Can you believe it? *Shrunk.*

My sister Natalie bounds into the room and we both stare solemnly in the mirror.

"If I pull in my tummy and you go for the zipper, they'll probably do up," I say hopefully.

I look at her reflected face. She's biting her lip, trying not to laugh, but she can't hide the mirth in those hazel eyes.

"Lie down," she orders.

"Why?"

"Gravity. It'll suck your tummy in."

"Oh, yeah? What happens when I stand up again?"

Nat giggles and makes wave motions with her hands in front of her enviably flat tum. It's okay for her; she's three years younger than me, has never had kids and runs five kilometres every day.

My mouth goes grim. "Muffin top."

"Maybe. But your blouse will cover it."

"Yeah, if I wear the white one that makes me look like a wedding cake instead of the slinky black halter neck."

"Don't worry, you've got great legs," Nat soothes. "I'm sure that will be the first thing Ed notices."

"Ed won't be there," I snap as I lie down on the floor. Nat kneels over me. I suck in my belly while she grabs the zip and wrangles. I hold my breath.

Zrrrrrrpppppp.

"Now, stand up."

I do as I'm told. They feel tight but not unbearable. The denim will give a bit, and if I don't eat anything all evening…

"He'll definitely be there," Nat remarks airily as she grabs the garment off the bed. It sounds suspiciously like she's been talking to Ed again.

"Don't be ridiculous," I snort. "He'll be leading a motorbike tour across the Kimberly or something equally stupid."

"Maybe it's time you two kissed and made up," Nat says.

I stare at the bulge of flesh over the top of my jeans.

It's nineteen years since I dated Ed. Nineteen years since the best relationship—and incidentally the best sex of my life—ended in tears.

"I'm a thirty-seven-year-old woman with two teenage kids," I say haughtily. "I'm not in the market for a quickie against the dunny door at the Class of 2001 Reunion. With Ed Cullen of all people."

Nat throws the flouncy wedding cake thing at me.

Her eyes are pure innocence. "Who said anything about a quickie?"

An hour later and I'm sitting at the bar of the Wallalinga Pub talking to Archer Greenwell. The same Archer who used to hide behind a swathe of unkempt hair and sinfully ugly glasses. I don't think I ever heard a peep out of him in class. He's wearing designer specs now and his hair is expertly styled. He's telling me all about his tech company in Melbourne. I'm busy sucking in my stomach and nodding at appropriate points in the conversation—well, to be honest—more of a monologue. From never saying a word, it now seems Archer can't stop talking.

My mind drifts. I wonder if I should check whether the twins are okay. I force away thoughts of my fourteen-year-olds, Evie and Rachel, having a sleep-over with six other hormonal teenage girls.

Just for tonight I don't want to be a mum.

I want to be the old Lacey. Before children, an acrimonious divorce and working for an arsehole boss wore her down.

The Lacey with a bright future ahead of her and stars in her eyes.

I take a slug of my second Margarita and waggle my eyebrows at my friend Janine in a 'come and save me' gesture. She winks back. Clearly, she thinks I'm having fun. My heart sinks at the thought of another hour of Archer.

A sudden commotion behind me; a roar of greeting from my ex-classmates, and I know for certain who's arrived. Ed was always the most popular kid in school. Why would that change just because he's on the downhill run to forty?

I give a final nod to Archer's description of his latest invention; a device that records your bodily functions and graphs them more accurately than a Fitbit, and swivel on my stool.

Frissons of electricity zap into every corner of my body, and I thank my stars I'm not wearing Archer's device right now because it would go off like a freakin' pin-ball machine.

My gaze glues onto broad shoulders encased in black leather and a face that's breathtakingly familiar. Deep-set blue eyes crinkle at the corners above impossibly high cheekbones. His jaw is ruggedly masculine, and he's sporting an almost beard that glints copper in the ambient light. As he moves through the crowded pub, laughing, hugging the women, slapping the men on the back, I see hands that are tanned and a little weathered. I see strong legs encased in leather bike pants and the flash of a white t-shirt against flat abs.

My heart pounds so loudly I'm sure it's drowning out the jukebox. His head lifts, and as though he knew all along I was watching him, his eyes lock with mine. Heat swirls around my belly, and honeyed warmth runs between my thighs.

Just with a look, Ed Cullen can do what he always did.

Which means…I'm still hopelessly besotted with the bastard.

ED

There's a heavy lurch in my chest as I catch sight of her at the bar.

Unmistakeably Lacey.

I'd know that tumble of dark blonde hair and those

soft, almost sulky lips anywhere. Maybe her figure's a little fuller, but that's the only difference. I should know; I used to stare at her often enough in class when she didn't think I was looking.

Suddenly she tosses back her head, and her gaze meets mine, dark and sultry.

That look. It always made her seem so mysterious…so out of reach…until we finally got together, and the sparks flew off the chart.

Does she remember how good it was between us?

Because I sure as hell can't forget.

Frankly, making love with Lacey was the yardstick against which I've measured every other woman.

My mouth is dry, my smile pinned on as I stroll towards her.

Don't rush it. Don't fuck it up, Ed.

"Hi Lacey."

"Hi, um—?"

Geesh, she's pretending she doesn't recognise me. Then a dimple appears on her right cheek and I breathe again. God, I remember, it was like striking gold when I got one of those smiles out of her.

"Ed, isn't it?" Eyelashes swoop over the dancing chocolate brown of her eyes; there's a tinge of pink on her cheeks.

"Changed that much, have I?"

"A bit." She shrugs. "The beard." She inclines her head towards her companion. "Remember Archer?"

I have to conceal my surprise. Scrawny little Archer of the 'every-day-is-a-bad-hair-day', looking tidy, and serious, and not a little put out by my presence. A stab hits my gut, and I realise I'm jealous. Stupidly, insanely jealous.

Archer shoots out a hand. "Pleasure to see you again,

Ed," he says. "I was telling Lacey about my company's newest product—"

As he rolls on like a road-train on a clear highway, I glance at Lacey. Her eyes widen back at me in exaggerated horror. A raft of memories kicks in; Ed and Lacey, all loved-up in our own little bubble. I reach out and touch her shoulder lightly. My cock bucks to attention. Suddenly I'm seventeen again and so hot for Lacey I burn up at night and pleasure myself until my arm aches under the shower.

She leans forward to put her drink on the bar and the movement wafts an intoxicating whiff of her perfume over me.

"That sounds fascinating," I lie. "Would you mind if I steal Lacey for a moment? We have a few years to catch up on."

Almost before the words are out of my mouth, she's off her stool, and I'm steering her gently by the elbow, her body bumping against mine and sending pulses to my groin. Out in the evening air, somnolent with the smell of dry earth and gum leaves, we collapse into nerve-fuelled guffaws.

"Oh, my! He's still Archer, only now at the extroverted end of the scale. I didn't know how to get a word in," Lacey laughs.

"Enough of Archer." I caress her with my gaze. "How are *you*? Since—?"

A sudden wall comes up in her eyes.

"How much has Nat told you?" she asks suspiciously.

Nat has always been my link to Lacey. Nat dated my cousin Hank for years and so I would get an update on Lacey whenever I could.

"I know your marriage broke up last year," I respond cautiously.

She tosses her head and stares out past the beer garden towards the stubble of harvested wheat. "It was over long before that."

As she leans on the rickety railing, I can't help but notice the fullness of her breasts under her flimsy silk top. I gulp hard and flick my eyes to the setting sun.

She says with sudden venom, "Andrew was a complete dick. And now I have a boss who's a complete dick." She gives a bitter little laugh. "Boy, do I know how to pick 'em."

It's pointed. I grit my teeth. Am I going to let her get away with it? The blame game.

No, fuck it, I came all this way to set the record straight. To stop both of us Facebook stalking each other, posting false, friendly Christmas greetings and the occasional veiled dig at each other. I came to erase the pain of seeing all those photos of her with her kids and socialising with her friends. There used to be pictures of her with her good-looking actor husband, but the fact he disappeared from her Facebook feed a year or so ago gave me the first glimmer of hope.

And I'm sick as fuck of being cast as the villain because she chose to misunderstand something that happened when we were eighteen.

"Are you including me in that description?"

"Don't flatter yourself."

My jaw tightens. She never gave me a fair hearing back then, even though I practically grovelled. I realised in the end it was convenient for Lacey to think the worst of me. It gave her the perfect excuse to leave.

Without looking at me, she almost snarls, "And how about you, Ed? Which pretty young thing are you fucking at present?"

I stare at her profile. I can tell she knows she's gone too far by the way her teeth rim her full lower lip.

"No one," I say quietly.

She clucks her tongue. "Yeah, right. I can see it perfectly—Ed Cullen kitted out in his bike leathers, pleasuring all those frustrated small-town wives."

"I call bullshit on that." She turns her head, and we glare at each other. "I've never been that kind of guy."

"The cheating kind, you mean?"

"Wow!" I sneer. "You could have built a career on being hard-done by. Truth is, you believed Tara's word over mine because it suited you. You wanted out of Wallalinga."

She gasps in outrage. "I left because of what *you* did."

"You left because you had a place at that pretentious drama academy. Which, incidentally, you chose not to tell me about. You fancied yourself as the next Nicole Kidman. And what did you get instead? Marriage to a B-grade actor, who only ever landed walk-on parts and toothpaste commercials."

Somehow. we're facing each other, poised to see who will land the next blow.

"You can talk—*Mr-no-fixed-address*, running dumb motorbike treks for sad, menopausal men."

"Nice one. I think I'll add that to my website," I drawl. "At least I'm happy." It's a barefaced lie of course, but by now the gloves are well and truly off. "Can you say the same? What happened to all your dreams, Lacey? Are you content with Mums-Ville and—what did Nat tell me you were working as? Oh, yeah, office manager for an ambulance-chasing legal firm."

"Bastard!" She spits, and her hand comes up. I'm sure she's going to whack me. Swiftly I lift my arm, and we meet mid-air in a parody of a Bruce Lee movie. My fingers curl around her wrist, and I feel the resistance in her crumble.

Maybe I give a tug, maybe she stumbles against me. I don't have a clue, but a moment later Lacey's slap-bang against my chest. Her soft curves weld to my body, and I'm instantly ram-rod hard. She grabs a fistful of my t-shirt, and our breath mingles, our eyes burning into each other like hot lava.

"Planning on using violence, were you Lacey?" I mutter, revelling in the scent of her hair, the glow of her skin.

Her lips are tantalisingly close, and involuntarily she licks them. She lets go of my t-shirt and both palms glide across my pecs and burrow inside my leather jacket, circling my ribs. Her breath smells of tequila. Our noses nudge, and then she presses her lips onto mine and I'm consumed by soft, wet warmth as her tongue forges into my mouth.

We kiss insanely, like two dying people stumbling on an oasis.

Finally, I groan, "Oh, Christ, Lacey."

She gives an answering moan of, "Oh, Ed—" as my hands roll over her hips, grip her butt cheeks and I haul her hard against my cock.

My lust-addled brain manages one last coherent thought:

This has been a fucking long time coming.

LACEY

I've turned into a tingling, melting pot of pure sensation.

If Ed wasn't supporting my butt in his big hands, I swear my legs would slide out from under me.

At the same time, my hands seem to have taken on a mind of their own, feverish fingers moving lower to tug at the buckle of his belt. Somewhere, in amongst his wicked tongue exploring my mouth and the feel of his cock pressed hard against my belly, a little voice is saying, 'For heaven's sake Lacey, you can't do *it* here…like this…' But it's drowned out by nearly two decades of rage. And regret.

And that's one heck of a combo.

I give up on the belt because Ed's thigh is now thrust between my legs, and I'm riding him. The tightness of my jeans adds an extra frisson of pleasure, the seam rubbing against my swollen clit. I never thought my jeans being so tight would provide an added advantage.

God, am I actually going to come? Humping Ed Cullen's leather-clad thigh in the beer garden of the Wallalinga pub?

I should be shocked at myself.

I'm not. I feel alive for the first time in years.

I don't even give a toss about my muffin top as one hand explores under the layers of white silk, glides across my stomach and cups my breast. Clever fingers shift the bra aside and twirl my engorged nipple into a hard pebble. I groan and grind every part of me into every conceivable inch of him. And then his head dips—and oh, glory—he's sucking my nipple into the heat of his mouth.

My head snaps back, my eyes abstractly taking in the darkening sky while animal sounds escape my lips.

A whirlpool of sensation swirls low in my belly. Yes—oh, yes…I'm about to…

The sound of quacking ducks trills through my teetering orgasm.

"What the——?" Ed's head appears from under my top, copper hair tousled, nostrils flaring.

"My. Fucking. Phone." I disentangle myself, fumbling in my back pocket whilst my breath comes in sharp, short pants. Ed is standing back, chest heaving, eyes dark with desire, and I'd love to throw the frigging thing way out into the bush, but I see the word *Angela* on the screen.

Angela, who has my girls staying at her house. Maternal worry freezes out the throb between my legs.

"Angela," I gasp into the speaker. "Is everything okay?"

"Sure. All good. You sound like you've been running."

I slump against the railing and glance at Ed. He's thrust his hands into his pockets, and I register the bulge in his leather-clad crotch with a spasm of pure want.

"No, no, just couldn't find my phone for a minute there," I lie, controlling my breathing with superhuman effort. "The girls——?"

Angela laughs. "They're having a ball. They want to meet up with some boys at the local pizza place. I'm happy to drop them and pick them up, of course, but I thought I should check with you first."

"Which boys?" I ask sharply. Ed's head is bent, but I catch the hint of a smirk.

"Elijah, Josh and another one who's name escapes me. They're all in the same class at school, apparently."

I scan my memory. "Elijah. That rings a bell."

By now shame is riding roughshod through my gut. I'm a *mother*, for God's sake, behaving like…like—*Shit!* if Rachel or Evie ever got up to this…I would…I would…

Horror rings the death knell to my libido.

"I've said I'll pick them up at nine-thirty. If you're okay with that?"

Ed has moved closer and is stroking little circles up and

down my arm. An involuntary shiver goes through me. I stomp on it.

What was I thinking?

That's the problem; I wasn't thinking, was I?

"That'll be fine, Angela," I say in a crisp voice. "Just text me when they're home and tucked up in bed."

"No problem." She pauses. "I'll let you get back to it."

I manage a squeaked, "Bye" as Ed nuzzles at the base of my neck.

Abruptly I pull away, shoving the phone back in my jeans pocket.

"What's up?" His voice is husky.

"My girls are meeting up with some boys."

"I gathered."

I feel stupid. Fat. Matronly. And not one bit sexy.

"This was a really bad idea," I say, not meeting his eyes. "I should go back inside."

"For fuck's sake Lacey, don't do this—"

I ignore the plea in his voice and yank my arm free. "Let's just forget it," I mutter before dashing back towards the noisy bar.

Inside, I grab my jacket and purse, ignore Archer's curious gaze and in seconds I'm running down the main street of Wallalinga, not daring to look back in case Ed is following me.

Finally, I slow. Heart pounding, I peer over my shoulder.

There's nothing but the deserted street lined with weatherboard houses, dwarfed under a sky fast filling up with stars.

Hot tears prick the back of my eyes, memories of the past swirling through my head. We'd been dating for a year when I walked in to find Tara Granger naked in Ed's bed. I always knew she had the screaming hots for him. She looked me in the eye and told me she and Ed had been fucking all night. Ed's story was quite different. Apparently Tara had turned up off-her-face drunk in the wee small hours and he'd given her his bed. He begged me to look at the sofa bed in the spare room as proof he'd slept there.

I didn't.

That same morning I'd got the acceptance letter from the Academy of Performing Arts in Perth. I was so torn, so confused. Loving Ed, staying here in this quiet wheat-belt town would mean giving away the acting career I longed for, and I just wasn't ready for that.

In my heart I think I knew Ed was telling the truth, but I worked myself into a frenzy; blaming him, throwing accusations and hurtful words, making sure I blew us to smithereens.

So I could follow my dreams.

Only to find that dreams can all too quickly turn to dust.

Don't get me wrong. I'll never regret having my beautiful girls. Not for a heartbeat. But—falling in love—happy ever after?

Just one big fizzle.

And to think I was almost stupid enough to open that Pandora's Box again.

I have no idea how long I walk around the streets of Wallalinga, berating myself, but eventually I'm standing outside the house I grew up in. The house where Nat now lives, teaching at the local school so she can be near Mum in the residential home. Even though Mum's dementia means she doesn't recognise either of us.

But hey, life was never meant to be easy, right?

Get a grip, Lacey.

I swipe the final trace of tears off my cheeks and walk up to the front door. In the kitchen, Nat's making a cup of herbal tea in her fluffy pink dressing gown. But that's not what grabs my attention. There's a black leather jacket slung around the back of a chair at the kitchen table. I know that jacket. I was hungrily exploring the body inside it a mere hour ago.

My mouth gapes open.

Nat grins at my shocked expression. "He's upstairs waiting for you."

ED

I hear the click of the bedroom door, and my shoulders brace.

I've spent the last five minutes standing by the window in Lacey's old room, telling myself this was a seriously dumb idea. But after the frenzied kisses we shared, I couldn't just ride off into the night.

It isn't over between us. It never was.

"Nat's a fuckwit for letting you in." There's a tremble in the voice behind me. The light flicks on and I turn, squinting at the sudden assault on my retinas.

Lacey closes the door and leans her back against it. Her mascara has smudged around her eyes, two big, dark craters in her pale face.

"Have you been crying?" I take a step closer.

"Nope." She's suddenly fascinated by her feet.

I take another step.

Lacey's head jerks up. "What do you want, Ed?"

I pause. Her breasts are moving rapidly up and down. My cock sparks at the memory of sucking her full sweet nipples, the feel of her heavy in my cupped hand.

"You."

She lets out a little bark of derision. I stare unblinking

at her and she doesn't seem to know where to look. But I feel her energy flowing towards me, around me, enveloping me.

Her lower lip wobbles. She slaps a hand over her mouth. Above it, her eyes are swimming in tears.

"Oh, baby." My voice cracks.

One more stride and I scoop her into my arms.

Her breath releases in an almighty *whoomph*; hands fly around my neck, fingers tangle in my hair as she brings her mouth into hungry contact with mine.

In a mass of arms and legs and lips, we tumble onto the bed, both of us crooning unintelligible noises, tugging at each other's clothes as we kiss.

She's yanking at my belt, the fly of my pants.

I'm struggling with the zipper of her jeans.

"Hell, were you sprayed into these?" I mutter thickly.

"More or less," Lacey giggles. "Don't ask." She places a finger on my lips. I suck it into my mouth in a gesture of what I intend to do to her shortly, and she lets out a gasp.

Finally, we're naked. I revel in every curve of her body as we press into each other, the softness of her skin against mine, the way we fit so perfectly together. Instinctively, I pull her on top of me.

"Oh, ahh—" Lacey sighs. This always was our favourite position.

Her thighs splay over mine, my cock nudges her entrance.

"Protection," she mumbles against my mouth as I cup her breasts and fight the urge to thrust deep inside her.

"Back pocket of my pants," I growl.

She moves off me and fumbles around on the floor, her bum thrust up in the air. I feast my eyes on her full buttocks, the patch of dark blonde hair disappearing into her cleft, and my balls ache fit to burst.

"Got it." Her eyes narrow as she scrabbles back next to me and waves the multi-coloured packet in the air. "Prepared were you, Ed?" There's a tinge of ice in her voice; a glint in her eye.

No way will I let her start another fight.

"I bought them at the servo on the way into town. Hoping you and I…"

She's still holding the packet away from me, frowning, but then she hooks one thigh back over mine and mutters, "Cocky bastard."

I burst out, "For fuck's sake, Lacey. The only woman I've ever wanted is you. This once, trust my word on that."

She hesitates, then her lips soften into a sweet upward curl.

"Okay," she murmurs as she straddles me. "Just this once."

We kiss again. Deep, drugging kisses. Together we tear open the foil pack. Lacey takes the condom and rolls it over my cock and the feel of her fingers around me nearly pitches me over the edge.

She lifts her hips and lowers herself onto my cock. It's the slowest, sweetest torture. Her eyes widen as she tightens around me, and she steadies herself with hands splayed on my shoulders. I move a hand down between us and find the hard bud of her clit buried between her wet folds. I circle my thumb pad over it as I thrust, knowing exactly what she likes, remembering every move that used to make her break apart in my arms.

She bites on her lower lip. Trembles. Moans.

We move faster, finding our rhythm. Her thighs clamp hard around my hips. Her clit swells under my touch, every move of her pelvis pulling me closer to heaven. She lets out sharp little mewls of pleasure, and her fingernails dig into my shoulder.

Sensation gathers at the base of my spine, tightening my balls.

I'm so fucking close.

I grit my teeth. I. will. Not. Come.

Not until she's right there with me.

Our eyes lock. "Oh yes, babe, take what you need," I pant.

With a long shudder, Lacey's back arches. "Ohh—Ed. Oh, fuck. Yes—Yesssss."

And now we're riding the wave; Lacey's orgasm sucking me deeper, spiralling me higher. One…two…three more thrusts and I'm coming so hard and furious I have no idea where the boundary between me ends and Lacey begins. I have no idea whether I'm hollering the walls of this old house down.

And you know what? I don't give a flying fuck.

Because Lacey and I are back where we belong. Together.

LACEY

Some indeterminable time later I'm lying with my head against Ed's chest, my fingertips drifting over the damp hair between his pecs. Neither of us have spoken since we came so spectacularly together.

Finally, Ed raises his head off the pillow; I look up, and he kisses my forehead.

"Guess we need to talk," he says.

I burrow back into him. "What about?"

"Lacey don't act dumb. Nineteen years of you avoiding me, save for the odd crumb on Facebook. Why would you never agree to meet me?"

I don't answer, but I don't pull away either. Lazily his

fingers play with my nipple, and seriously, I could go in for round two.

"I can't resist a man in leather. That picture of you on your website…" I give an off-key wolf-whistle. "I knew I'd jump your bones if we met up."

He frowns. "Come on, Lacey. The truth."

"That is the truth. In fact, why don't you put those pants back on so I can rip you out of them all over again?"

He hunkers up on an elbow and searches my face. "You know I've never stopped loving you, don't you?"

I try to look away. I can't. I'm pinned by the post-coital clarity of his eyes. I nod. The jokes shrivel on my lips as the words *I never stopped loving you either*, bubble up inside me.

"I came back to see if there's a chance for us." He traces my jawline with his thumb. "Now that you're finally free of that dickhead husband."

I should say it's too complicated, I should say it won't work; not when Ed's away for months at a time with his outback travel business. Except, maybe that's not such a bad thing, considering my circumstances.

Before I can answer there's a sound of ducks quacking. I dive for my phone and read Angela's message. *The girls are tucked up in bed. Enjoy your evening.*

I slump back on the pillow. "I have too much baggage," I say, but my tone is unconvincing, even to me.

"I'm used to carrying baggage. And riding through rough terrain. I'll cope with whatever you throw at me."

Ed's leaning over me, his eyes shining with lust and something so much deeper. "Give 'us' another chance, Lacey."

I gaze into the face I've missed so much. What if this is my last chance at happiness? What if I let it pass because I'm too shit-scared? Will I live the rest of my life with even more regrets?

I throw caution to the winds. Crush the fear. Then I wind my fingers into Ed's beautiful thick hair and bring his face close to mine. "Maybe we should see where this ride takes us."

"Guess I'll accept that for starters." Ed's grin turns X-rated. "Right this minute, I've got another kind of ride in mind—"

And as we lose ourselves in round two, it occurs to me that some dreams do get a second chance after all.

The Real Thing

GEORGIA MOORE

Vanna comes out of the simulation breathing heavily. She takes ten seconds to freak out, then activates the touch-screen in her training pod and runs a malware scan. It comes back clean.

"Damn."

Despite the result, Vanna's instincts tell her something is wrong. She thinks back to second year and sets up a more advanced scan. It takes longer than she likes. Computronics is her weakest area.

The progress bar jumps 1% at a time. Too slow. It doesn't distract Vanna from the buzz of adrenaline under her skin. Of arousal.

Vanna thumps her head against the seat in her training pod. She shouldn't have let the faulty simulation go on for so long. As soon as the AI appeared as Leon, she should have shut it down.

She closes her eyes and recalls in vivid detail the AI-Leon, his lean torso wrapped in his supple leather sparring uniform.

She clenches her legs together. "Don't do it. Don't do it," she chants like a mantra, her body singing for touch.

She takes slow breaths in and out.

The progress bar is only halfway.

Groaning, she pushes out of the pod and steps across the hall into her tiny bathroom to splash cold water on her face. It does nothing for the heat inside her.

In the mirror, her reflection betrays. Cheeks flushed and pupils so dilated there's barely any brown.

"Leon?" she judges her reflection. "Really?"

Vanna braids her long black hair, assembling a hydro-gun part by part in her head to calm herself. It's one thing to have a sex-dream while her subconscious is in control, and another to consciously decide to kiss Leon—and almost more—while fully awake. Even if she was inside a simulation and it wasn't really him.

Her pod *pings*, scan done. She pulls the back panel out into the quasi-corridor between the pod and her bathroom so she can see the screen while standing in the hallway.

She skims the analysis and scoffs. "All clear?"

Kicking the side of her pod doesn't change the results.

Vanna shoves the panel back in. She knows something is wrong. She wishes the instructors were on base so she could get Sergeants Chandra or Jeong to run a test. But they'd been called up as emergency reinforcements after the latest counterstrike and aren't expected back for another week.

Vanna groans. There's only one person on the base who matches them in skills. Only one person who can help her figure out what's wrong with her pod.

Leon König.

As she jogs around the space station, Vanna can't help feeling she's missing something. She lines up the facts. It's the first time in three years Sergeant ranks and above have been off base at the same time. And it's the first time her pod has malfunctioned, in fact she's never heard of it happening to anyone.

It's too coincidental. It must have been deliberate.

Plus, her training AI didn't just appear sentient, it turned into Leon. If he's accessed her pod, he has her logs, progress stats, personal memos and a dozen other things that would give him a foot up in their three-year-long battle to top their cohort.

The conclusion helps nudge her lingering arousal closer to anger as she finally finds Leon in the corridors behind the archive rooms.

"Hey! Leon!" Vanna shouts.

Leon lifts an eyebrow as Vanna stops in front of him.

"What the hell did you do?" she demands.

Leon grins and slips his hands into his pockets. "Vanna. A pleasant greeting, as always."

Vanna doesn't dignify it with a response. "What. Did. You. Do?"

"The way you're asking makes me not want to answer."

Vanna thinks about pushing him against the wall. She's not sure physical contact with the real Leon is smart while there's still a thread of arousal pulsing through her.

"You did something to my training pod," she accuses.

Leon cocks his head. "Come again?"

"My training pod. You tampered with it."

"No, I didn't."

"Oh, come on." Vanna throws her hands in the air. "With the instructors away, you're the only person on this ship who could."

Leon's smile is too big for friendliness. He's enjoying himself. Vanna's skin prickles.

"Is that a compliment?"

Vanna ignores the teasing question. "You telling me you didn't jump at the chance? I know you hate me."

Leon stiffens. His mouth turns down for a second before the smile slips back into place.

"I have no idea what you're talking about," Leon dismisses Vanna's anger, leaving her itching. "Besides, I've been pulling overtime in the archives. When would I have had time to tamper with your pod?"

Vanna clenches her fists, wanting Leon to meet her anger, fight back. She has the horrible thought it's driven by the need to touch his skin.

"You're saying you couldn't do it?"

"I could," Leon assures. "But I didn't."

Vanna narrows her eyes.

Leon steps toward her. She hates that she had to tilt her chin to maintain eye-contact.

"What would I gain from tampering with your pod?" he asks curiously.

Vanna swallows, thinking of what she and the AI-Leon were almost doing. She hopes he attributes her heated cheeks to racing around the space station, not embarrassed horniness.

"Nothing."

Leon hums. Vanna sees the tilt of his head and knows he's thinking about possible reasons.

"Sorry. I didn't mess with your pod," Leon eventually says. "Like I said, I've been working overtime. Check the logs if you don't believe me."

"I will. Don't worry."

As Leon moves away down the corridor, Vanna exhales shakily, feeling like she lost an argument they barely had.

Stalking back to her pod after checking the logs—Leon was telling the truth—Vanna is back to square one, except somehow more frustrated. As authentic as the simulations are, they've never perfected the olfactory. Leon's musk-and-ozone scent feels like it's lodged itself in the back of Vanna's throat, sitting on her tongue all the way back to her room.

There's probably a grey area with what Vanna's accepted she's about to do, but now she knows Leon will never find out, she's horny enough not to care. Plus, maybe after this she'll stop having dreams about Leon, nightmarish fantasies where she devours him with frenetic, hurtful hungriness, and confesses feelings she definitely doesn't have.

She climbs into her pod and goes into the faulty simulation again.

AI-Leon stands sunlit in the grassy field of Vanna's simulation, leather pants clinging to long legs and padded jacket unzipped over a tight singlet.

"You came back," AI-Leon says with a smile Vanna has never seen in real life. It's fond.

"Don't sound relieved," she says, unsettled. "You don't like me, remember?"

"Actually, you're the one who doesn't like me."

"I don't not like you. I just don't like you."

The emotional chit-chat is not why Vanna is here. Her skin buzzes. A voice in her head asks if she's really going through with this.

Vanna moves. She's six steps from Leon. She's doing this. One time to get him out of her system.

"I don't not like you either," AI-Leon says.

"Great. Can you talk less?" Five steps. "I get enough of

that in reality."

"But how will I ask what you want?"

Four steps away, Vanna falters. The heat in AI-Leon's eyes is disarming.

"How will I ask what feels good?" Leon continues, voice deep. Goosebumps break out along Vanna's skin.

"How can I tell you how insane you make me every time you wear that?" Leon gestures to Vanna's uniform. Leather grips her from ankle to wrist bone. She gulps in air, chest pushing against the zipped jacket.

Leon steps in. Every nerve ending tingles, and he hasn't even touched her. She never feels this way in her dreams. Is this because she's cognisant this time?

"How can I chant your name as I come if you don't let me speak?" Two steps away.

Vanna's stomach twists. She tries to sound firm when she speaks. "Fine. You can talk."

"Maybe later," Leon says, taking the final step and kissing her.

The fervour of his lips takes Vanna by surprise. She stops thinking about real-Leon verse dream-Leon verse AI-Leon. Vanna stops thinking.

Leon's lips are on her neck. His hands unzip her jacket and slide under her t-shirt to press hot on her back. He walks her backwards until she bumps into one of the anomalous oak trees and it hurts for only a second before Leon's lips are on hers again. Vanna sinks her teeth into Leon's lips and in return, Leon's tongue flicks inside her mouth and drags over her teeth, tasting her. His hair is thick between her fingers and the heat between their bodies builds until the leather sticks to her skin.

It's the desperation of years of animosity spilling over, yet Leon's hands are gentle as they push her jacket from her shoulders.

"Vanna," Leon whispers right into her ear. "What do you want?"

Vanna shudders. She's giving herself this once so she can move on from her attraction to Leon, stop getting those stupid dreams. But how can she have all the things she's dreamed in this one moment?

"Should I take my time?" Leon keeps talking, kissing down her neck, dragging his teeth over her skin while Vanna's pulse trips over itself. "Should I use my fingers? My mouth?"

Vanna can't think. In all her dreams, Leon's been quiet. It's the point of difference between dream-Leon and real-Leon that made them bearable. It wrecks her to have AI-Leon talk so much, so like the real thing.

It wrecks her because she's revelling in it.

Leon returns his lips to hers and asks against them, "What do you want?"

His eyes burn bright and Vanna's pulse thuds at her core.

She pushes his jacket roughly down his arms, then strips his singlet off his body before doing the same with her own shirt and bra. Leon grins. She puts a palm on Leon's bare chest and forces him back a step.

Leon is pale everywhere, even the trail of hair disappearing into his leather pants is a barely there blond. She's seen it before—the harsh V of his hipbones and the sharp definition of his torso. The bulge in his pants is new. He doesn't hide, but his expression is almost bashful. Another dissimilarity from dream-Leon.

They're both breathing heavily. The itch blooms under Vanna's skin again.

"What do I want?" she repeats Leon's question. "I want to come on your tongue," Vanna tells him, voice rumbling out of some deep, private part of her, body clenching in anticipation.

She pulls him back to her, pressing their chests together. Heat everywhere. "I want you on your knees."

Vanna's hands slide down Leon's back and around the hem of his pants. She presses her palm down over his erection and Leon's eyes flutter shut. He swallows a moan. It makes Vanna giddy.

"Then I want you in me," Vanna tells him, "giving me everything you've got so I feel it when I get out of this simulation. So I can stop dreaming about you."

"You dream about me?" Leon asks, eyes opening.

"Yes," Vanna half-groans, "but did you hear anything I said before that?"

Leon retrieves his jacket from the ground and slips it behind Vanna's back. "You should put that on."

She shrugs into it as Leon drops to his knees. His jacket sits heavy on her shoulders, still warm.

"I heard you," he looks up devilishly. "I always hear you. You wanted something like this."

Leon isn't gentle anymore. He tugs off her leather pants and throws them away. When he puts his mouth on her over the lace, he doesn't hold back. Vanna spreads her legs, tremors running through her.

Leon's always been verbose, but he's phenomenal using his mouth this way too. Vanna's hands grip his hair. She has one leg over his shoulder, relying on him and the tree to keep her upright. Leon pushes the lace aside and runs a finger through her folds as he tongues her. He slips the finger inside. Vanna groans, and a spasm moves through her, pleasure starting in slow waves. Leon adds another finger. The waves get closer together.

When Leon stops, a groan rips from that private part of Vanna that Leon's been coaxing to the surface.

"How much do you like these?" Leon asks, voice rough. He snaps the side of her underwear. Her eyes fly open as the sting resonates outwards and her nipples peak.

"It's a simulation," Vanna growls. "I don't care. I really don't care. Tear them off."

Leon does.

Leon's tongue is magma hot and pinpoint accurate, licking over her in alternating flicks and long strokes. Vanna's never been this loud before. She doesn't know if it's the privacy of the simulation or that it's Leon. And she doesn't care. She can't care as Leon's fingers press against her g-spot and he sucks hard on her clit and doesn't let up.

Vanna comes in a wave of continuous release, body curling forwards, hands holding Leon to her until it hurts, and she has to let go, leaning back against the oak trunk, grateful for Leon's jacket. Leon moves her leg off his shoulder and sits back on his thighs. Vanna feels like sin and Leon looks as bad with his mussed hair and shining mouth. He unbuttoned his leather pants at some point and Vanna can see the tip of his erection, an angry red poking from his briefs.

She's on her knees, straddling him in an instant, hands reaching for his skin. This is the one time she's giving herself this, and she's taking all she can.

Leon's hand travels up her front, cupping a breast and kneading. Her nipples are hard already, and she pushes into him, wanting the friction. His thumb rubs circles over one and then Leon's mouth is on the other and Vanna's back on the high-wire, body electric.

She pushes Leon down onto the grass and strips him of his leather pants and black briefs. She should stop to look; she knows she should. This is the one time she gets to have this, but even having come already, the itch persists. She needs Leon's skin again. She takes what few seconds she can, notices the muscles in his legs, a birthmark high on his left thigh. Then she's on top of him, straddling him, feeling him press hot by her hip.

"Is this my dream?" Leon asks. "You in my jacket on top of me. You going to ride me, Vanna?"

"Is that what I said I wanted?" she replies, sucking at the juncture of Leon's neck and shoulder, circling her hips until she feels the length of him pressing right where she wants it.

"You said you want me in you," Leon repeats her words.

Vanna grins and grinds down hard. Leon's groan sends a shiver up her spine. Vanna does it again, and Leon's hands grip her hips.

"I said," Vanna speaks between panted breaths, "I want you to give me everything you've got."

Leon flips them. "You want to feel this later?" he asks, slipping two fingers back inside her. They go easy and she clenches around them.

A third finger and it's good, but not enough.

"Leon," she groans, moving until her legs are locked around his waist.

"I get it," Leon tells her before finally filling her up, moving in with one, slow push. Vanna's breath catches. "No more talking."

Leon moves slow and deep, starting a rhythm Vanna matches quickly. She can't stop touching his hair, even as he moves his head from her lips, trails kisses down the centre of her chest, moves across to a breast and sucks. Vanna's quivering as Leon gives her himself. His cock and hands and mouth. His thumb rubs her clit and his thrusts turn shallow, brushing over and over at that sweet spot inside her.

Leon chants her name as Vanna clenches around him.

She's a breathless mess, pleasure moving through her in waves, bigger and more powerful as Leon meets her desperation until Vanna's a tsunami unleashed, her orgasm pulsing out from where their bodies are connected.

Leon's forehead presses to hers, his eyes screwed shut. She tries to notice everything at once, to satisfy whatever part of her keeps dreaming of Leon so it will go away.

"Vanna, Vanna," Leon chants.

Vanna clenches around him, kisses him until Leon's mouth goes slack and she can feel him coming inside her, pulsing his release.

Spent, Leon draws back to look at Vanna, expression returning to fondness like when Vanna first re-appeared in the simulation. His fingers brush her lips.

Something stirs in Vanna's chest and before she can pinpoint what it is, she pulls out of the simulation.

The bliss doesn't last long. She told AI-Leon she wanted to feel it when she came out of the simulation. She definitely feels something. Her skin still buzzes, and her heart feels strange.

She can't use her pod again while it's like this, especially when there's a part of her thinking about going back in already. She tries showering the thought away with scalding water, changing on autopilot into her sparring outfit after. She has to fix her pod today, which means she needs Leon.

He's easy to find at a desk in the archives.

"I've been thinking all afternoon about what I could gain from hacking your pod," he says conversationally, eyes fixed on his data pad.

"Well stop. I need your help."

That gets his attention. His eyes lift to hers, inquisitive. Vanna feels an echo of heat. So far, having sex with AI-Leon hasn't had the desired effect.

"Vanna Spinelli." Leon's lips curl up slowly. "First a compliment and now you want my help."

"Don't make this a thing," she warns. Even after showering, she wonders if he can see lingering signs of pleasure on her cheeks. "I need help with my pod."

"That again?" Leon's voice sours. "I didn't mess with your pod."

"I know. You said so and I believe you. Whatever." Vanna barrels past the admission that Leon was right. "But you're the best at computronics on the space station right now and I need this fixed. Today."

Vanna waits for Leon to tease her. Instead, he unplugs his data pad, standing up even as he asks, "What's in it for me?"

Vanna's chest lifts with relief. "Pride at solving a complicated issue?"

"You know me well."

"Wish I didn't," she says while asking herself how that happened.

The first thing Leon does is run the same tests Vanna already tried, even after she tells him so. She puts space between them, moving to the table in her kitchenette instead of criticising him. It's a marked difference from how she would've reacted yesterday, facilitated by an unprecedented moment of hesitation when she thought about insulting him.

Leon's pulled the pod's panel into her hallway, but she can see him through it. He strips off his jacket as his tests run and throws it into her pod. Knowing his jacket is in her pod where she had sex with AI-Leon makes her chest feel fluttery. She swears she can smell the leather mixing with his musk-and-ozone scent even from the back section of her room.

"Nothing's coming up," Leon says.

She rolls her eyes and tells herself she's only imagining the scent. "I told you that."

She stays at the table for the next twenty minutes while Leon works, attempting to refine sketches for a new surge dampener, but Leon's frustrated exhales break her concentration with increasing frequency.

"You want food? Coffee?" she interrupts when Leon's last groan sounds reminiscent of the noises AI-Leon made. He's so vocal all the time. It's a wonder it never featured in her dreams.

"Uh, okay. Yeah." He sounds surprised by the offer. "Coffee, thanks."

Vanna makes it and brings it over.

"Scans aren't finding anything," Leon says, pushing the panel into the pod so there's room for Vanna. "Is there sugar in here? I normally—"

"Two cubes. Yep."

Leon's hand stalls, and Vanna has to push the mug into his palm. She brushes past Leon and sits in her training pod where she hopes her flushed cheeks are hidden. Why does she remember how he takes his coffee?

She shouldn't have gone into the simulation a second time. It's messing with her head.

Vanna's half-sitting on Leon's jacket. The leather-musk-ozone scent is real now. She hooks her fingers into a sleeve and feels a pulse in her abdomen. This close, Leon fills her field of vision. She can't stop looking at his fingers and imagining them inside her.

"Tests are done."

Vanna startles.

"I even did some not-technically-sanctioned ones. Nothing."

"Maybe you're not as good as you think," Vanna replies in her usual style, hoping her body will get the memo to stop reacting abnormally to Leon.

Leon laughs, taking a sip of coffee. "I am. But I don't know what I'm looking for. Why won't you tell me the exact issue?"

Vanna steals his coffee instead of answering.

"Okay. Don't tell. But when I figure this out, you won't be able to say I'm not as good as I think."

Leon focusses back on the panel, his deft fingers typing lines of code she can barely decipher. His competence, normally so infuriating, is for once on her side. The effect is very different. Vanna clenches her legs together.

"What're you doing?" she asks to distract herself.

"I'm going to play back your session archives," Leon explains.

"Wait!" she yells, dropping the coffee and trying to stop him. She wedges her body between Leon and the panel. It's futile.

There's no sound, but Vanna knows the playback has started because Leon's eyes widen. Vanna's blood rushes in her ears.

"That's…We're…"

It's the first time Leon has ever been speechless. He recovers quickly.

"You're into me," Leon says halfway between a question and a statement of fact.

Vanna has no hope of hiding her blush.

"You're six-foot and toned and you've got good skin," she tries responding logically. "But attraction doesn't mean

I want that to happen in real life." Vanna is telling herself as much as Leon.

"You don't?" Leon's eyes travel over Vanna's face. "Your pupils are dilated."

"Shock."

"Shallow breathing. Shaking hands," he adds.

"Also signs of shock. See?"

"But—" Leon pauses. His exaggerated breath feels deliberate as their chests push together. "I can feel your nipples through our shirts. I think if I—" Leon pushes up, chest dragging over the sensitive buds. Vanna whimpers.

"See?" he throws the word back in her face. "You would want it in real life."

Vanna can't deny at this moment at least, she wants. Their lips are so close. For a crazy moment, she's sure Leon is leaning in, but then he steps back, and she's left unfulfilled.

"Don't worry," he says. "I wouldn't do anything while you hate me."

Vanna swallows roughly. "I don't hate you."

Leon scoffs. "Doesn't feel that way."

"Well, it didn't feel like you hate me, either," Vanna counters, looking obviously at Leon's crotch.

Leon's reply is long-sufferingly, heavy with exasperation. "That's because I don't hate you."

It's Vanna's turn for shock. "You don't?"

"Vanna. You're smart. Driven. Confident. And your lips make me—" Leon cuts off. "Like I said, I'm not having sex with someone who hates me. My self-esteem isn't that low."

Vanna itches, annoyed she's so breathless, annoyed Leon is touching her one minute and not the next, annoyed he's not listening to her. Annoyed that even after sleeping with AI-Leon she can't get him out of her thoughts.

"I don't hate you. You frustrate me," she hisses, pushing off the panel. "You're egotistical about your talent. And you make friends easily. Whenever I hear your voice, I can't ignore it. Your hair is so stupidly blond I spot it the second I walk into a room." She digs an angry finger into his chest on each point, yet the more she talks, the more she hears what she's saying, realising something she's been ignoring for years. Why does she know his damn coffee preference?

It's not only in this moment she's wanted Leon.

"I don't hate you," she repeats, flattening her hand against Leon's chest.

His heartbeat thrums beneath her palm. She's seen that look in his eyes.

Even knowing it's coming she still gasps when Leon's lips meet hers. This is the kind of kissing Vanna dreamed; desperate.

"Vanna," Leon whispers into her ear. "What do you want?"

Vanna is breathless. "The AI-Leon did the exact same move."

Leon's hands slip from her body. Vanna misses them like an ache.

"Of course." Leon's hands fist in his hair. "The oak trees. They're mine. I should've noticed."

Vanna guides his hands back onto her body. She's finally admitted why she's been so obsessed with Leon and he's stopping? She licks up Leon's neck, wanting his musk-and-ozone in the back of her throat like she couldn't get in the simulation.

Leon groans and shudders against her. "Vanna, I know

what's happened. It's a new AI-model I've been working—"

Vanna grabs his face, kissing him hard. "You wouldn't stop talking in the simulation either."

"I can fix your pod," he insists.

Vanna puts her fingers over his lips. "Later. We're in the middle of something. Or did you miss that?"

Leon stills, and Vanna knows she's pushed a button.

Leon traps her against her pod, shoving a thigh between her legs.

"Of course I didn't miss it," he growls, grabbing her ass and grinding her against his thigh. Even through the leather Vanna feels blistering heat. "I've only been imagining it happening since you called out Sergeant Dreyfus for misquoting the New United Nations Treaty."

"That was first year."

"I know," Leon's teeth graze the shell of her ear and Vanna whimpers. "You've been driving me insane ever since."

She shoves Leon over to her bed, stripping his shirt off and unbuttoning the leather pants, pushing them down his legs. "That was first year. First year."

Leon's hands tug her top over her head and then his lips are on hers, his nimble fingers unclasping her bra. Vanna pushes her pants off and kicks them away. Naked, they tip onto the bed and Vanna ends up beneath Leon. He kneels between her thighs and the hard length of him glides through her folds and presses her where she aches. She arches into him, hands grabbing his biceps, as he kisses her mouth, her chin, her collarbone. All the while moving his cock against her clit, spreading her wetness and turning her insides into an inferno.

"Do you know how jealous I am," Leon confesses

roughly, "of a damn AI of myself? That he got this before I did?"

Leon's teeth graze her nipple and Vanna jerks. "You get the real thing. Trust me," Vanna says, shuddering as a hand grazes her inner thigh. "It's better."

Leon's fingers move through her folds, gathering her wetness, using it to slip two fingers inside her as his thumb rubs her clit in torturous circles. Vanna drops her head back on the pillow. Leon's blue eyes watch her. It's nothing like AI-Leon or dream-Leon. It's better. It's real.

Vanna yanks him down and rolls them over so she's on top. She stretches for her bedside table to grab a condom, then rolls it over his length as his fingers play with her nipples, making her shudder and twitch. Making her sweat, making her clench around nothing, ready, so ready, for this to happen.

She wraps her hand around him and sinks slowly down. Leon's skin is the pinkest she's ever seen it. He fills her with blazing heat.

"Vanna," he says, reverent.

She steadies herself on his chest and moves, building quickly into a rhythm. Leon plants his feet on the mattress, and Vanna is tilted forwards, falling onto her forearms. They kiss hungrily as skin heats and sweat builds and Vanna's body thrums, everything tightening. Her breasts rub against Leon's chest and when she spreads her legs further and takes him deep, there's delicious pressure on her clit with every upward thrust.

"I need—" Vanna gasps into Leon's mouth.

Leon slips a hand between them and touches her where she wants it. Vanna goes taut, pleasure climbing somehow higher before Leon's thumb rubs her clit harder and her orgasm rushes out, sparking along her nerves, an earthquake followed by endless tremors.

Leon swears as Vanna comes. She's still shuddering from the force of her release when he grabs her hips tight and hammers into her with ragged thrusts. She tries to meet him but there's no rhythm anymore, no finesse, just need. Her name falls from his lips, and Vanna watches him come apart beneath her.

———

"Where're you going?"

"To fix your AI," Leon tells Vanna, propping himself up on an elbow and reaching over her for his shirt. "You don't need him now," he adds, amusement in his eyes.

"Don't be an ass." Vanna tugs the shirt from him and throws it across the room.

"You wanted your pod fixed today," he reminds her.

"You've wanted me since first year."

"You're fixating. Is this a pot-kettle situation?"

Vanna should do some reflecting on what Leon is implying at some point. After the buzz under her skin dissipates. If it ever does.

"Maybe," she gives Leon.

Leon rolls his eyes. "Maybe."

"Take it or leave it," she tells him.

"I'm taking it. Many, many times."

Vanna catches his expression before Leon kisses her. Fondness. God, how did she miss what their tension has really been about.

As Leon's tongue glides over her lips, there's a flutter in Vanna's chest. She doesn't hate the feeling.

Heart Magic

KRISTIN SILK

In the deep quiet of the forest, I pause above the body. I say my usual hunter's prayer, thanking the creature for its life, then slice the rabbit open at the belly. Carefully removing the skin, I lay it on the grass. The soft fur and dried leather of the pelt will make a fine blanket to repel the winter's chill, when added to the other skins I've collected.

I poke a stick through the carcass and prop it over my fire between two branches. My belly rumbles mutinously. It's been a day and a half since I last ate. Enough to make the hunger sharp.

I trim the rabbit skin, throwing offcuts into the bushes for passing creatures. I'm so hungry I want to eat the whole rabbit but force myself to wait. The raw meat will make me sick.

The moon is full as the last of the light falls into shadows. It is a big moon, a harvest moon. Its energy vibrates inside me and through the forest.

Hunger must have dulled my senses because I almost

miss it. The snap of a branch and a shadow leaning towards my dinner cooking on the fire.

I launch myself at the shadow, hoping there is only one. On connection, the shadow becomes flesh and bone. So solid, I struggle to push it down. A man, by the looks of things. A thieving man out to steal my dinner. He grunts as I hit him and knock him to the ground. We roll. He doesn't give in easily. Nor do I.

I straddle him and try to pin his arms, but he is too strong and rolls us again, until he's on top.

"I mean you no harm." His brown curls fall forward as he looks down at me.

I didn't get to be one of the best hunters in my clan by believing fairy stories like that. I push against him. He presses my arms into the leaf litter.

"Stop fighting."

I'll stop fighting when I'm dead. But I pretend to give in. He immediately releases my arms. I whack him on the side of the head and wrestle until I'm on top.

"Who are you? What do you want?"

He blinks, stunned. His green eyes shine up at me in the firelight. Then he fights back, rolling us again until we are perilously close to the fire. His body holds me down, from chest to toes. I wriggle and am met with a wall of unyielding muscle.

He holds my wrists. "Please, stop. I won't hurt you."

Then he rolls us away from the fire, so I'm on top. My thighs bracket his hips. He stares at me for the longest time and I stare back. His gaze burns deep into mine and my breath leaves me. What strange magic is this?

I don't know what's happening to me. There's a burning sensation in the centre of my chest. Energy sparks through me, and fire fizzes in my veins. *Pull back, Xanthe. He must be a sorcerer.* But I can't. I'm helpless against the pull of him.

When he reaches up and caresses my cheek, I'm caught, like a rabbit in a snare. His thumb traces my bottom lip, leaving a trail of tingles, and my heart pounds.

Firelight dances in the darkening pupils of his eyes. His lips part and I trace them with my fingers. He stares at my mouth. The fire in his eyes flares and makes me burn.

I know only one thing. "I want you."

"Yes." His voice is deep and husky, his eyes drunk with longing.

It's all the invitation I need. His lips taunt me. I can't stand it. I lower my mouth to his.

He responds instantly, his mouth hungry on mine. Ravenous. Desperate. Need explodes inside me. I slide my fingers into his hair. His hands glide over my body and the hunger for him is sharper than for food. His hardening arousal fuels my need. I press my hips against his, and he groans.

"Yes," he murmurs. "Oh, yes."

I'm not alone in this. We are both possessed. We kiss and kiss, desperate hungry animals. Starving. Drowning in need.

I claw at his clothes, pulling and tearing at them.

He laughs. "Easy."

I make a noise of utter desperation. He slides his hand beneath my leather tunic and over my bare behind, and I lose my mind.

Clothes are the enemy now. I rip and tear at the material that keeps him from me. He pulls my leather top off, rips the soft cloth underneath. We claw at each other's skin, hungry, relentless.

I kiss and bite his neck. His insistent fingers find their way between my legs, sliding in the slick wetness there. I moan, grateful now for the contraceptive implant we were all forced to have fitted. At the time I thought it was stupid. I'm a hunter, not one of the soft ones, making babies and goo-goo eyes at a man.

Now I say a silent prayer of thanks as I slide him into me. He fills me perfectly and I pause to kiss him deeply, drunk on arousal, intoxicated by the taste of him.

He groans, and the sound vibrates through me. Then he pulls me tight against him, his hands stroking my body, setting off sparks inside me.

My hips take over then, sliding over his skin, grinding into him, hard and fast. My blood beats a rhythm in my head. *More, more.* I'm a slave to the dance of our bodies.

The pressure tightens in my core, building higher and higher, tighter, and tighter until bliss borders on pain. I don't ask for the pleasure. I take it. And in taking my own, create his. His breath labours in my ear. Then it hits and I cry out, my body tensing and convulsing as pleasure seizes me in waves. I tighten around him, wringing out every drop of exquisite sensation.

He rolls us so he's on top and thrusts deep inside me. I thought I was done. I don't know how, but I'm building again. His gaze is deep and intense as it locks with mine. I wrap my legs around him. My fingernails claw at his back. My fevered brain watches helplessly as our bodies take over. He thrusts deep, again and again, hitting the secret spot inside me until I explode. My eyes roll back in my head and I let out a deep, keening moan.

It's as if my other orgasm was just a prelude. This one blows me apart. He explodes with me, thrusting deep one last time as he stiffens, groans and shudders against me.

We clutch at each other, spent, breathing like we've escaped danger. He lifts himself onto his elbows and stares into my eyes. He kisses me deeply, then pulls out of me.

We rouse ourselves, and I crawl back from him. How could I have let my guard down so badly? It could have been fatal. I know nothing of this man I just had inside me. He could have been a Shadowling. I shiver at the thought.

He grins lopsidedly. "Well, hello."

He looks from me to himself and chuckles. Our clothes hang in tatters. We look like we've been attacked by wild animals. He reaches out a hand to me.

"I'm Rhyder."

I shake it, which seems ridiculous after what we've just done, and stare at him. What magic is in those eyes? How did he make me lose my mind? He must be a sorcerer.

He's still holding my hand. "And you are?"

"Xanthe."

It comes out croaky, like I've been standing downwind from a fire.

He smiles, and my heart leaps in my chest.

"Pleased to meet you, Xanthe."

I seem to have swallowed my tongue.

He clears his throat. "I wasn't going to steal your dinner. I was only going to ask if you'd share it with me." A pause. His face falls. "Hell."

"What?"

"We didn't use protection."

"I have an implant, and we have regular health checks."

"I've never, you know, without protection, so I should be good."

I nod. It's a little late for this conversation. Arousal is fading and fast being replaced by embarrassment. I rummage for my ruined clothes and pull them on as best I can. He does the same.

As we feast on the rabbit, I struggle to understand what just happened.

"How did you do it?"

I stare at him over the fire. The flames cast gold highlights in his brown hair, which curls to his shoulders.

"Do what?" Those green eyes look so innocent. What magic is this?

"What spell did you use? What enchantment did you put on me just now?"

His eyes go wide. He shakes his head. "No spell. No enchantment."

"Then what? You can tell me. I won't be angry." I have to know.

Confusion clouds his eyes. "I don't know what you're talking about."

My eyebrows knit together. I don't want to say it aloud. "I mean, you know, what just happened…"

"You think I bewitched you?" He laughs, a deep, rumbling sound that scrapes low in my belly.

I nod. Damn him. "Just tell me how you did it."

"I promise you; I did nothing."

He looks earnest, but I'd be a fool to trust him. I've already been foolish enough.

When he asks to share my camp for the night, I point to the other side of the fire. "You stay over there."

After what just happened, I'm not taking any more chances.

The next morning, as Rhyder follows me back to the compound, I sift through my memory to explain the previous night's behaviour.

"It was a full moon. All kinds of magic happen at a full moon."

He raises his eyebrows doubtfully at me. A leather pouch hangs from a strip around his neck. A-ha!

"What's in that pouch? What talisman? What magic?"

He takes it between his fingers. "It's for protection." He laughs quietly. "Though it didn't protect me from you."

I kick a fallen branch out of the way with unnecessary force. There must be an answer.

He keeps stride with me. "You still can't accept you were crazy for me, can you?"

My cheeks and neck burn with heat. In the light of day, I can hardly bear to remember how out of control I was.

He catches my eye with a cheeky grin. "If it makes you feel any better, I *am* pretty irresistible."

I growl and step faster. Of all the possibilities, that is the least acceptable.

At the compound we are greeted and taken to medical. Orin's eyes grow wide as she takes in our clothes.

"What happened?"

I make a strangled noise before I recover. "Got caught in some prickly bushes."

I hate lying. I never do, but there's no way I can admit what really happened.

Orin peels off Rhyder's top and examines his back. "Oh. That's nasty. You've got some deep scratches here."

The memory of my fingernails clawing at him has my cheeks heating up.

Rhyder grins, knowing Orin can't see his face. "I came into contact with a wildcat."

I almost choke as he winks at me. I leave the room to compose myself.

When Orin's finished with him, I return.

"You know," she says casually. "Those scratches looked a lot like fingernails. You wouldn't know anything about that, would you?"

I freeze. Mortification swirls through me. But I've always trusted Orin. Maybe she can help. I clear my throat twice before I can speak.

"I…don't know what came over me. I think he used some enchantment. I've never felt or acted like that before."

Orin considers, in her thoughtful way. "I detected no magic on him."

This is bad. "But…but how?"

Orin is quiet for so long I don't think she'll answer. "Maybe it is a kind of magic, but not the kind you're thinking of."

"What do you mean?"

"I mean the magic of the heart."

I stare at her in shock. "I don't even know him."

She pokes at my arm. "You still have the implant?" I nod. "Good." Her grey eyes are serious as she places a gentle hand on my shoulder. "The magic of the heart is a powerful thing. No one is immune to love." She looks away then, so sad and wistful that I wonder who she's thinking of.

I shake my head. "I'm a hunter, not a breeder. I've no time for love." Just saying the word makes me cough.

"Then make time."

"It wasn't love. It was two animals rutting. Why are you filling my head with these ridiculous ideas? It was carnal, pure and simple."

"So, you wouldn't care if he was with someone else tonight?"

My whole body stiffens. My fingers clench into fists. "Why are you asking this?"

"Relax, Xanthe. It's just a question."

I shake her off. I'm done here. I stand to leave.

"Xanthe?"

"What?" My mood has soured like curdled milk.

"You're a hunter. Love might be exactly what you need."

I snort. All this talk of love has me wanting to place an arrow between the eyes of the next person who mentions it.

"And how do you figure that?"

"When you're in danger, having someone to live for isn't such a bad thing."

I blow out an irritated exhale.

Orin picks up the broken leather of my tunic. "Funny."

I glare at her. "What now?"

She returns my stare with a calm poise I will never possess. "I never picked you for a coward."

I grit my teeth and stalk from the room.

———

At the banquet that night, I sit opposite Rhyder and try to ignore his existence. He's getting a lot of attention, especially from the females. One server approaches him. Kirralee is all soft curves and pale skin, with a waterfall of golden curls tumbling down her back. I push my fingers into my own short, dark hair. Functional, not pretty. She fills Rhyder's tankard with wine and smiles at him, fluttering her lashes. I curl my toes against the leather of my sandals. When Rhyder smiles back, I fight the urge to rip Kirralee's throat out with my bare hands. I grind my teeth together.

Rhyder catches me watching and heat flares in his eyes.

When another server offers him bread, I can't stand it. The thought of him being with another woman makes me want to tear myself apart.

I've been so long hunting I've become a wild thing myself. Maybe that's all it was last night. I'm tired. That's all. I will go to my chambers and lie down. I scoff my food like an animal and leave.

Laughter and voices rise and fall in the background. I'm halfway to my chambers when I hear footsteps behind me. I turn. Rhyder steps towards me. He's dressed in a clean white tunic like me. His hair is freshly washed, and he smells so good. I breathe in and get lightheaded.

"Where are you going?" he asks.

"To bed."

"Want company?"

I should say no. I'm about to, but instead I'm grabbing the material over his chest and pulling him closer. His lips fall to mine as his hands grasp my waist. He kisses me deep and hungry and I whimper like a wounded animal. I wind my arms around his neck. He strokes up my side, splaying his fingers so they ripple along my stomach on the way up. He cups my breast, and my nipples peak. The kiss deepens as he changes the angle. Our tongues slide together, hot and wet. My brain clicks off.

I reach for him, sucking in a breath as I take his hard length in my hand. I slide my fingers up and down, and he groans. He reaches down, slides his palms under my behind and lifts me. I wrap my legs around him. I try to take him into me, but he resists.

"Wait."

He carries me into his bedchambers and lies me on the bed. We shuck our clothes into a pile on the floor. He leans over me and kisses me deeply. I reach for his cock again.

"Wait," he gasps.

"You don't want to?"

He gives me a lopsided grin. "What do you think?" He guides my hand to his rigid cock. "Of course, I want to. I just want to take things slower this time, make it good for you."

I stare up at him, his green eyes mesmerising. His lips trail over my mouth, my neck, my collarbone, my shoulder. Achingly slowly, he teases me until I can't stand it. He covers my breast with kisses and sucks the nipple into his mouth. I arch against him and moan. He presses my nipple between his tongue and the roof of his mouth. I cry out as a corresponding zap of pleasure hits me right in the core. His mouth works on one breast while his fingers toy with the other. His hands are gentle but sure. He is simultaneously arousing and soothing me.

The flood of sensation is overwhelming. Rhyder continues his torturously slow expedition down my body, worshipping me with his tongue. He settles between my legs, sliding his fingers up my inner thighs until I tremble. His fingers trace over the soft curls between my legs, setting off sparks all over my skin. He parts my folds with his tongue and my head falls back.

"Oh."

He slides a finger inside me, then another and licks me slowly and luxuriously, as though he's eating something delicious and never wants to stop. His fingers keep a slow, steady rhythm and his tongue lifts me higher and higher until I am floating in clouds. I'm unravelling under his touch, falling apart piece by piece. I'm not sure how much more I can take. Need spears inside me, twisting me tighter and tighter until I cry out.

I'm dangling on the edge, perilously close to release.

"Oh. *Oh*."

My orgasm is so close I can taste it.

With an anguished cry, I break. He caresses my hips as I shudder beneath him. I'm stardust bursting and floating in the far recesses of space. He slows but continues until the aftershocks fade.

He crawls up my body and kisses me deeply. My thighs open wider in welcome and he eases himself into me, starting our rhythm with slow, lazy strokes. Nothing has ever felt as good as having him inside me. My hands feast on the muscles of his back as they glide beneath my fingers. Stroke after stroke, he loves me until I am rising again. This slow, gentle thing is a different beast altogether from the wild rutting of our first encounter. His gaze sears into me as though he sees all of me.

For the first time since we met, I'm not afraid. I see him too, through time and space. We are locked in a moment of union so sweet my throat tightens. Then he smiles, easing me through it, taking me with him to bliss. I follow willingly. My heart swells, and every part of me reaches out to hold him, body and soul. He's going so slowly, waiting for me to catch up.

His eyes ask the question. Holding back is getting increasingly difficult for him.

"Yes," I whisper, and his eyes catch fire, igniting me until we are both burning, a blazing inferno, higher and higher.

Our bodies take over then, moving together fast and violent, desperate with the need for release. When he shudders and moans deeply, I follow him over the edge, holding him tight because I am never letting go.

He sags against me for a moment, then kisses me gently. He moves beside me and pulls me close. The tenderness in his eyes is followed by a fierce flash of possession. It's like looking in a mirror.

"You're mine." His whisper is urgent.

I stroke his cheek. "You're mine, too."

We kiss, sealing the promise of our hearts with our lips.

I stare at him for an age. "Are we crazy?"

He shrugs. "I should have let you know."

"What?"

"That I felt the same, that first time. It was like magic for me, too."

I fall asleep in his arms, lulled by the warmth of his breath against my cheek.

We haven't spent a night apart since we first laid eyes on one another. The rest of me has finally caught up with what my heart knew immediately—that he is mine, body and soul.

Now, Shadowlings have been seen five miles north of the compound. Too close. As I check my arrows and place them one by one into my quiver, I remember Orin's words. *Having someone to live for isn't such a bad thing.*

I'm not so sure. I'm nervy and distracted. The thought of being apart from him is unbearable. The only time Rhyder forgot his protective leather pouch was when he injured his leg on a routine hunting trip. So, now I make sure he wears it every day. Unfortunately, his wounded leg means he can't come with me. He hates it and has sworn next time he'll be by my side.

When it's time to leave, he's nowhere to be seen. Maybe it's for the best. Maybe saying goodbye is just too hard. Maybe it's better this way. We've skirted around words of love. It hasn't seemed necessary. I scan the crowd of well-wishers one last time, then turn with the other hunters, away from the compound.

"Xanthe!"

Rhyder limps through the crowd. "Take this." He pulls his leather pouch over my head. "For protection. You need it more than I do."

I curl my fingers around the soft leather. "Thank you."

He pulls me so tight against his chest I can hardly breathe. "Please come back."

I hold tight to him, inhaling his scent, knowing I will need the memory of him to keep me going. I nod.

His eyes are wild and scared. "You must come back. I love you."

My heart leaps. Of all the times to tell me. But maybe it's the perfect time.

"I love you, too."

Our lips meet in a deep, fast kiss. I take one last look into those mesmerising green eyes and walk away, with the other hunters, into a danger we do not yet understand.

The last thing I see is a pair of glowing eyes. I fire an arrow at the Shadowling and gasp as I am hit in return. The arrow pierces my chest, above the heart. Searing pain blasts the breath from me. The world tilts and slows. I fall to my knees. Someone is dragging me. My fingers curl around the leather pouch. All I can think of is Rhyder. I must come back to him. How will he know that with my last breath I thought only of him?

The world smudges and goes dark. I float above my body. So light. I am weightless. I see Rhyder. I float towards him. His face is contorted with pain as he falls to his knees. He pulls at his hair and screams my name. "Xanthe!" Over and over. He is sobbing. He knows I am dead.

My love, I'm here, I tell him, but he cannot hear me. I try to reach him, but an invisible wall separates us. I float away, and then there is nothing.

In the tomb-deep silence, Rhyder's words echo. *You must come back. I love you.*

I want to clutch the leather pouch he gave me, but I cannot find my way back to my body. In my mind I weave a rope towards him, made of love, made of leather, made of light. I cling tight to the rope with only one thought. *Do. Not. Let. Go.*

I open my eyes, blink, and everything blurs together. It is white and still. I am in the afterlife. My eyelids close.

Rhyder's voice is soft and urgent. "Xanthe, my love. Wake up."

I do not know how I can hear him, but I don't want it to end. The floaty feeling dissipates, and I gasp as pain throbs through my body. I try to move my mouth, but no words come out.

"Take your time."

It's Orin's voice. How is she here? Where am I?

Finally, I croak out some words. "Am I dead?"

"No, my love, but you came very close to it."

I open my eyelids a crack. Rhyder's face swims before me, lined with worry. And there is Orin, her expression grave and serious.

Rhyder smiles at me. "I knew you could do it. I knew you'd come back to me."

"What happened?"

"You were ambushed. Half the hunters did not return. You almost died." Orin's eyes are sad.

A wave of grief for my fallen fellow hunters hits me. "No."

Rhyder gently squeezes my hand. "Don't think of that now. You need all your strength."

I'm as weak as a newborn rabbit. I can't move my arms. I close my eyes again.

"Rest, now." Rhyder's voice is tender as he presses a soft kiss to my temple.

When I wake sometime later, Orin is beside me.

"Rhyder?"

She pats my arm. "I've sent him to rest. He hasn't left your side since you arrived a week ago."

A week? How have I survived a week and not known it?

As if she can read my mind, Orin says. "We first got news that you were dead. Then the remaining hunters arrived, carrying you. I thought you were in the afterlife. I don't know how you lived. I've never seen anyone survive the wounds you sustained."

Rhyder's love was the lifeline I clung to, when I was drifting, when I thought I was dying. My eyes fill with tears. "Rhyder."

Orin's eyes go misty and her tone is gentle. "What did I tell you? Having someone to live for is not such a bad thing."

My chest hurts, and not just where the arrow pierced me. I am overwhelmed by my love for him. When he appears at the doorway, tears stream down my face.

"I love you."

I want to say it over and over until the day I die. I want him to *know*.

Orin discretely disappears, leaving us alone.

"I love you too, my brave warrior." Rhyder strokes my hair. "Rest now. I will be here."

My fingers go to the leather pouch around my neck, as they often do, of their own accord. Rhyder sits behind me, his arms around my waist. My back sinks against his chest, and his breath tickles my ear as he kisses my neck. He is wearing the leather pouch I made for him out of rabbit skin, over his heart, for protection. My wounds mean I can no longer hunt. The thick scars over my chest remind me how lucky I am to be here, watching the sun rise on another day, in between the legs of my beloved.

I cradle Rhyder's head and stroke his silver hair. We have weathered many seasons together, and our skin is lined with experience. I pull the blanket made of rabbit pelts over him. The leather is worn soft with age. His eyes don't open. His breath is soft and shallow.

It won't be long now.

I stroke his hair gently. My love has taught me many things. How to love when I would have run. How to hold on and live when I was close to death. But how do I learn what he teaches me now? How to love enough to let go.

Orin moves quietly. All that could be done, has been. There is nothing to do now but wait.

Orin pauses at the door. "He seems to be holding on. Maybe he needs to know it's okay to let go."

I absorb her words, and my chest throbs. He has never wanted to leave me. I must be brave enough for both of us. When the door clicks shut behind Orin, I lean to kiss Rhyder.

"I'm here, my love. But you must make your journey alone. I will love you always, beyond space and time. It's safe to let go." I swallow the lump in my throat and kiss his forehead. "I love you."

He squeezes my hand, so faint I could have missed it if I wasn't paying attention. I squeeze back. He lets out a shuddering exhale and then, stillness. The moment is filled with love, with reverence.

He does not breathe again.

<hr>

I have lived a good life. I have loved deeply and well. I am not afraid of death. When I close my eyes for the last time, the peripheral sounds recede until there is a deep stillness and a single point of light. I follow the point, like a tiny star, and leave the heaviness of my body. The light becomes brighter. Letting go is so easy, so filled with peace, that I am grateful this is what Rhyder experienced.

I am weightless and free. A shape moves towards me. A figure. It's Rhyder, looking like he did when we first met. We understand each other without speaking.

My love, I have been waiting for you. The love that shines from him fills me with light.

My love.

I look down at myself, young too. We both wear our leather pouches. I touch my fingers to his. He smiles and reaches for me. The joy in his eyes stretches into eternity. *And now we have forever.*

I now know for sure what I have always suspected, hoped—that true love never dies.

Sweet Treats

Want to try something a little sweeter?
Why not try our Sweet Treats Anthology?

In 2020 we refreshed our Little Gems competition with a
new theme with the brand of Sweet Treats.

Sweet Treats 2020:

CUPCAKES

Think of all those yummy treats that make you feel good,
or that you might get or make for your loved ones.

The theme for the 2020 Spicy Bites anthology will be...

DENIM

For details of how to submit a story, please see Romance Writers of Australia's website http://romanceaustralia.com/contests/aspiring-contests/ spicy-bites/

Previous Spicy Bites anthologies can be purchased from the Romance Writers of Australia store http://romanceaustralia.com/shop/

About the Authors

Kristine Charles

Kristine Charles loves telling sexy tales, exploring relationships between complex women and the strong men who love them, then working out just how much pain to inflict, or not inflict, before giving her characters their HEA (or, at least, their HFN). She writes, and reads, to escape into other worlds where coffee (and red wine) is abundant, designer shoes and handbags are cheap, chocolate has no calories and men always put the toilet seat down. Find her at wordsbykristinecharles.com or tweet her @wordsbykc.

Karen Lieversz

Karen Lieversz is a writer of quirky stories and poetry who has a kink for injecting spice wherever she can. She thrives on pushing the boundaries to see what lies beyond and hidden within. Karen is close to finishing (so she thinks) her first full-length novel, a contemporary women's fiction, exploring the conundrum of death-bed confessions.

When Karen isn't writing, you can find her hitting the dance floor with her husband or walking her crazy kelpie cross through the bush.

More details, including anthologies where Karen has short stories published, can be found on her website: https://www.karenlieversz.com

Cordelia Fox

Cordelia Fox is a History teacher at a traditional, conservative secondary school in New Zealand. She loves writing steamy sex scenes and uses a pseudonym so she doesn't alarm her teenage students. In 2019 she set herself the challenge of writing a novel. Although it hasn't been published (yet) Cordelia found the experience so enjoyable that she is partway through a second novel and has plans for two more. Her other passion is academic study and she wants to undertake a PhD in History. Alternatively she may work on becoming fluent in Spanish and go and live in Cuba.

Samantha Marshall

Samantha is an author of speculative fiction who has been living stories as long as she can remember. She lives in Melbourne, Australia, with her husband, two children, one fluffy golden retriever and a turtle. Everywhere she goes, Samantha sees magic and mystery and all of the incredible things that are both real and imagined, which she pours out through her fingers in the form of books. She is most at home in front of her keyboard with a hot cup of chai tea and a little dragon sitting on her shoulder, and can be found online at www.sliceofsammy.com

J A MacNally

Jan and writing have enjoyed a life-long love affair, starting with the first SF story she wrote in primary school. Her background (English teacher and communications officer) has helped hone her writing skills, as shown in autobiographical short stories, some published in anthologies. She shares her passion for cinema and literature by writing reviews for online websites, e-newsletters and her blog. She enjoys wearing SF costumes at pop culture conventions along with her family, reading extensively, collecting soundtrack music and anything related to the incomparable Jane Austen, who first hooked her on romance.

Web: https://suchreviewsaboutnothing.wordpress.com/author/suchreviewsaboutnothing/

Instagram: https://www.instagram.com/karls.girl/

Novalee Swan

Novalee Swan is the Amazon bestselling author of six novels and novellas. She writes paranormal and contemporary romance. Her *Shifter Town* series features sexy alpha shifters and small town charm, and she has recently launched the *Sin City* series, set in Las Vegas. Novalee reads too much — is that possible? — likes pretty things and jumps at any chance to travel.

Web: www.novaleeswan.com

Facebook: facebook.com/novaleeswan

Celeste Darling

Growing up as an avid bookworm of everything from sci-fi/fantasy to old school bodice-ripping romance, Celeste has always enjoyed the opportunity to bend narrativium to her will throughout multiple genres. Her present focus is on getting a few more erotic short stories out, and writing a longer novel (or three). She plans to do this in between professional work contracts, serving two furry gods in feline form, crafting with fabric, and tending to her kitchen garden. She can be contacted on celeste.x.darling@gmail.com and would love to hear from you.

I M Jasper

I M Jasper is a late comer to romance. Initially drawn to the love and enticing predictability of happily ever afters, the genre delivered a delicious escape from reality just when it was needed the most. She lives with her husband and enjoys daydreaming about travelling, drinking tea and curling up with a good book, especially on a cold day.

Julie Holland writing as Allegra Stone

Julie contributed erotic short stories to monthly magazines (back in the day when erotica was delegated to a bookshop's bottom shelf, if stocked at all), then drifted to other genres. She is a current writer of contemporary romantic fiction novels. Julie weaves stories around heroes and heroines who are strong, yet vulnerable; who haven't lost their sense of humor or their desire for a great sex life. An erotic novel is simmering, gathering heat and magic, under one of Allegra Stone's many hats. Facebook: www.facebook.com/juliehollandauthor

Davina Stone

Davina Stone writes romance with heart, heat and humour. Her short stories are featured in several Romance Writers of Australia anthologies, both spicy and sweet. Davina devotes her time to talking to her plants, finding excuses not to exercise and honing her romance writing skills on the beautiful West Australian coast. Her first novel, a sexy sweet rom/com will be published in early 2021. Join her for free short stories, updates and links to her social media platforms on https://www.davinastone.com/

Georgia Moore

Georgia Moore has been a lover of romantic fiction since she realised she read every book waiting for the romance storyline to appear. By day, Georgia edits cookbooks and by night (and bus rides and in the middle of dinner) she writes. Contemporary and paranormal are her favourite romance genres. When not consuming copious amounts of—sometimes questionable—pop-culture, Georgia can be found attempting a new cake recipe, playing tenor horn in her community brass band, singing in the Sydney Philharmonia Choirs or being overly competitive at board games.

Follow Georgia on Facebook and Twitter @GMooreWriter

Kristin Silk

A long-time student of human nature, Kristin Silk has loved writing from a young age. Although a late comer to romance writing, she has found her happy place in the world of happily ever afters.

Kristin writes relationships based on respect and equality, with a dash of humour and a side order of sizzle. She is inspired by kindness, courage, love in all its forms, and people who bravely live their own truth.

She resides in picturesque central Victoria with her husband, daughter and one very squeaky guinea pig.